Unbuttoning Light

The Collected Short Stories of
Mattie McClane

Mattie McClane

Myrtle Hedge Press

Unbuttoning Light: The Collected Short Stories of Mattie McClane
Copyright © 2012 by Myrtle Hedge Press
245 Rockford Road
Kernersville NC 27285

ISBN 978-0-9722466-4-4
Library of Congress (LCCN) 2012932041

To my mother

Stories are not linear; they are hierarchical, like seats in theaters, with levels, main floors, box seats, balconies, just as an auditorium. In its seating, are poses, all the faces of history.

How should you be? What do you want?

The gallery of onlookers clamor; there are on one level, the bodies of kings, robed in satin, jeweled crowns, rubies and emeralds.

There are the English Georges, six of them, carefully arranged. George III, with his moonlike face, shakes a fist at the American patriots across the way.

Patrick Henry lips his reply, "If this be treason, make the most of it."

Generals are seated in rows, rustling their swords. Who indeed has the largest sabre? They are a noisy lot. Their elbows clash; they want more room.

Their medals jangle.

Their horses line the aisle, panting, clawing, resting, beside valets and blacksmiths.

Above them are poets and scholars, dreamers, who read books and raise an occasional eyebrow.

Beside them are the faces and glamour of Hollywood— James Dean, doing his own impression.

Musicians break into discordant song. One plays a flute as if he were making a cobra rise from a wicker basket. The trumpet player awakens soldiers asleep in their chairs, and they reach for their guns.

This is knowledge.

Explorers unfold maps. They fidget. They spin their globes and remember weather, billowing clouds, damning winds. Crates are behind them packed with the booty of other places, remembered scents of dried exotic flowers.

This is desire.

Contents

Unbuttoning Light

A Mood for Thinking in Threes

"Are we ready to go?"

"Not quite," my mother said.

I looked at my mother who, for a moment, looked like an aged version of Lana Turner costumed for mourning, a black suit and matching hat, strung with a mesh veil. My sister's eyes secretly groaned at her appearance, and sought my own for a solution, as if our family had fallen mysteriously ill, waked up with painful joints, and could not venture any further than a nightstand for warm milk and medicine.

We could not possibly attend the funeral.

My mother took a few items from a large purse and placed them into a black clutch.

"Did you bring a hat or a veil?" She stood, came close to me, adjusted my collar, pulled my blouse evenly, so it fell outside my jacket.

"No," I said.

"Do you want one of mine?"

"Not really."

"I set those out for Martha." Mother pointed to several hats on the table, a heap of finery, feathers, ribbons, pearls, and shining beads.

Martha sighed.

I took one that looked like a gray bird beak and placed it on my head. "What do you think?" I bent over to look into a mirror on the buffet. I stooped, put my face in front of Martha, hoping to make her smile.

"Great, just great," Martha said.

"It's backwards; turn it around." Mother took a pin from a bag, walked over to me. "It goes like this." She smoothed my hair behind my ears.

"No hat, Mother."

"I'm not looking forward to this," she said.

Martha nearly said it then, gently, ever so gently, some kind of suggestion that Mother could stay home and rest. I both frowned at Martha and winced at the alternative. The picture's preview was in full motion in both our minds, Lana Turner in a tear-jerker and heads would turn, the heads of church committees, the heads of Avon ladies and knitting aunts.

But, of course, she would not cry.

I dangled my keys in front of Martha as signal that it was time to go, and she sat on a chair with her hand on her temple as if a headache centered in her brain. After a moment, she stood and reached for the tissue box on the buffet, stuffing a few sheets into a pocket.

My mother took me aside and said, "This is going to be difficult for Martha."

Martha began to whimper in the backseat of my Volvo, and Mother watched the highway from the passenger seat seeming to ignore the sounds behind her.

Mother's dress came off best in places like Palm Springs, Estes Park, Aspen. On sidewalks, tourists often asked her to sign autograph books. She would smile, always flattered, and explain that while she used to sing, she was merely the wife of a country judge in rural Iowa. The tourists blushed, stared at their feet, rocked from side to side, and then told my mother that she really did look like somebody.

Martha sobbed.

I decided not to look at either one of them, and occasionally glanced out the side window to take in the landscape, rocky, hilly pasture, with a few trees growing in the background, all seemingly planted in threes. I began to think in threes, and how many things came in threes, three little kittens; three Christmas magi; Roosevelt, Churchill, and Stalin at Yalta; table settings, knives, forks, and spoons.

For three decades, for I am thirty, I have been familiar with this highway, leading to my late father's hometown and grandparents' home.

The *Niña,* the *Pinta,* the *Santa Maria.*

In the backseat, as a child, with Martha, I pretended that the hills were giant ocean swells, and I was Del Cano sailing around the Cape of Good Hope. Surviving mutineers were my crew, and water lashed out at my ship. I was the first to circle the world on a vessel named *Victoria.* Magellan, now lost, had been my captain, and we set out in search of cloves and rich spices not previously known in Spain.

Harcourt, Brace, Jovanovich.

I learned that in a library, reading biographies, stories of great men, because the stories of women then were not great. I thought that about Betsy Ross, a seamstress who was visited by George Washington, and about how the two had differed over the number of points on the original flag's stars.

Betsy said five. The president wanted six. Ross won out for an unexplained reason and prompted a biographer to write a child's book.

Betsy Griscom: Born in Philadelphia in 1752, married the upholsterer John Ross, remarried twice after his death, worked as a seamstress, had seven children and died, 1836.

I turned to my mother and back to the road. I caught a glimpse of Martha in the mirror, still crying.

I wished that I was Del Cano again, skipping this scene, a wish that made me sense a kind of vague cowardice in bold dreams. The water was still now, and the sun's brilliant heat annoyed me like the buzz of insects, and my ship was motionless. I stood. I staggered. I predicted the sky. I was captain and needed to be silent about my fears.

That was Del Cano.

It was not me. I drove my car into the church's gravel parking lot. My mother frowned at the white dust. Martha recovered herself from a slump and took an audible deep breath. My grandfather was dead, I thought to myself for the first time on the trip. How odd.

Mother's narrow heels slipped on the rocks, and she walked ahead of us.

The Father, the Son, and Holy Ghost. A man asked us if we were friends or family. Martha said family, and we were escorted to a front pew near the altar. The bench was full, seating cousins, their spouses, an uncle, a couple of aunts by marriage. We were ushered to the back of the chapel, far back where the carpeting stopped and turned into tile: Folding chairs replaced the heavy pews.

"I'm very sorry," the man told us. Mother straightened a chair. Its metal scraped the hard floor. My sister's hand was once again on her temple.

I was between them.

I thought about how little I knew about my grandfather and about grief. Mourn death, grieve something real, like childhood, smells of wet leaves and sand near a river, adults talking or giving out soda. A huge turtle shell, minus its creature, was in a bucket by the path.

I thought about the path. I turned to Martha. Red circles puffed around her eyes, and she wouldn't look at me. So I returned to the path, a linear groove, marking the course of rainfall down the hill. At the bottom, there was a mud bank and it defined the shore of a brown river. A tree was uprooted. Its spike-like roots formed a great round, and as a child, I imagined that it was the head of Medusa.

Three Gorgons. Medusa, the only mortal sister of the Gorgons, had been proud of her hair. She boasted of her beauty to Athena and changed into a hideous creature, fangs for teeth, protruding eyes.

Then the wind would gust, causing ripples. A blue sky would put a part of itself down on the water, so the murkiness might disappear, no silt, now an ocean. I sailed away from the image, having no desire to be turned into or to turn others into stone. Without a shield, I was not Perseus.

My mother put her hand on mine.

Martha was sort of gasping, choking. Mother was still. I adjusted myself on the chair. I squirmed. I did not like my place in the middle now. I wanted to tell Martha to sit up straight. I wanted my mother to cry. I wanted to stand, excuse myself, exit a meeting that had gone on too long. Pardon me.

Pardon me. I could check my watch, frown, and leave others with the feeling that they had wasted my time. I could do that if this were a meeting. I could fiddle with my pen, page through hours of testimony. I could say I have listened and I have watched, but I still do not understand. My patience has been tried, Martha, and I cannot grieve your estranged grandfather. Nor mother, can I act out your dispassion or even tell if it is real. Forgive me, but I have an appointment.

In the parking lot, after the services, my mother and my uncle John exchanged a cordial nod, standing back from each other. Men huddled and scurried around the back of the hearse. I watched cars line up behind it.

I walked over to John, hugged him, released him, seeing familiar eyes, dark, slate-like. "Your father would be pleased. I've heard you're involved in politics," he said to me. "Politics in Iowa."

Indicative. Imperative. Subjunctive.

Would. Could. Should. If I were king. It seemed to me that all the possibilities for grief were contained in this mood, all the pondered alternatives for reality, every well-created scenario, every if and would be.

"Thank you," I said.

My mother took my uncle's hand, squeezed it. "I'm sorry, John."

Martha began walking toward where we had parked. Mother followed her. I wanted to stay behind, for a moment, wanting to wait just a little longer before joining them.

Playing
by the Rules

"And when the heavens open'd and blazed again
Roaring I saw him like a silver star—
And he set the sail, or had the boat
Become a living creature clad with wings?"

—*The Holy Grail*

Jimmy was strapped into a lifejacket and looked like a package, ready to be mailed, a bow, shoelace style, was tied underneath his chin. I sat beside him on the center bench of a rowboat.

I must have looked the same, all wrapped up, like no sailor, no captain.

I pulled on the strings beneath my face, deciding not to wear the jacket. My arm went behind my head and lifted it. It caught my ears.

Jimmy watched, seemed to think my move was pretty daring, not because I might have drowned without it, but because he imagined that the judge would find out.

"I can't wear it," I told him.

Jimmy smiled.

I raised my oar, turned to my brother, and we were off, going up river, past summer cabins, to where cottonwoods were thick, casting green on the water, as if a shiny fabric was placed on its surface.

I saw Jimmy's oar rise and fall, with mine, two oars, and we'd pull together, lean far back, go forward to catch the next wave, and our common effort seemed important, like a mission, full of urgency.

Jimmy stopped rowing, turned to me. "Let's quit for a while," he said.

He lifted his oar, and we continued, moving the boat upstream.

Every explorer had had a time like that. Somebody had wanted to quit and then decided to go on, too much water had been sailed, and it was too far from home, and waves leapt over the bow, and the situation was scary, dangerous, and maybe the sailor was tired.

Maybe Balboa wanted to turn back on his trip, but was urged on by Bastidas.

Explorers claimed things, brought back gold, and Vasco Balboa had married the daughter of an Indian chief at Darien. My book didn't tell her name.

I watched water drip from my oar, and the drops fell like melting diamonds.

My brother pointed to the shore, wanting to rest, tie up to the branch of a fallen tree. And I wondered why she was mentioned at all.

Balboa had a wife. It was like old McDonald had a farm, and no more.

Balboa had stood on a mountaintop, seeing an ocean, and he named it the South Sea, said its coasts belonged to Spain, but the woman he married was not remembered. I looked at Jimmy, and now he seemed like a captured elf, and I fastened a scratchy rope to the limb.

The branch was broken, but not separated from the tree; white splinters stuck out from the break. Jimmy moved to the front of the boat.

"We need to bring something back."

Jimmy cocked his head, asking what.

He turned, looked at the trees, the mud banks, then said, "Nothing to bring back."

But on the shore, between the branches, in the weeds, was an object that appeared to be a box. I lifted myself onto the tree trunk, walked along it.

"It's a soap cabinet."

Jimmy frowned.

"It won't float."

"Maybe it will," I said. Last weekend, in front of Jimmy's friends, I bet that a container, the kind that electric workers stood in, would float, and spent maybe a half hour trying to talk somebody into getting in it; nobody would, I did, and it sunk.

Jimmy didn't understand my wish to make boats, but he didn't know many stories, only the ones I told him, about Hudson and Champlain, people who found things. My brother knew rules, instructions, what time to be home, how to hang up a rake, and I thought that was good; we imagined different things, but still I thought I might convince him that stories were rules, like a law, our father's instructions, things were always done in the same way.

Whether he believed me or not, he went along with me. I told him the story, and he'd pretend it with me. He'd be anyone for me, and I didn't always give him good parts; that was the best thing about Jimmy.

"Please," I said, turned backed to my brother. And he looked at me for a long time, then pulled at the tie to his lifejacket, needed to take it off to come up onto the branch. From the perch, he saw what I wanted to tow, wasn't impressed, but conceded.

"It looks like a canoe."

Jimmy's eyes were interested.

I wanted to tell him that it was Balboa's wife's canoe, felt a real desire to have the soap cabinet be hers, the daughter of an Indian chief may have lost a boat, but that would mean making up a lot.

It didn't matter whose canoe it was, I thought. I jumped down from the limb. My shoes stuck in the mud, and I lost my balance, falling forward. My brother threw me the rope,

I tied it to the brace underneath and the tan speckled shelf. What did an Indian woman do?

Why might she need a boat, and how did she come to lose it? The knot was tight.

I sat on the branch, kicking back globs from my shoes, then returned to Jimmy.

We rowed away from the tree, pulling the aluminum cabinet at an angle, and finally it came to the edge of the water. I looked at it; its ends were square, and if we kept rowing, water would come over the top of it.

"We'll have to float it back."

Usually, now, after we had tied onto something, I'd tell about people in my books.

The cabinet lagged behind, its seams were broken, and it was heavy from the leaks.

I picked up my lifejacket from the floor of the rowboat, fussing with the straps, stringing the thing around my neck, fastening it at my waist.

Jimmy gave me a funny look, seemed to laugh at me all tied up in an orange pillow, and he knew we were getting close to where the judge picked us up. Just for that, I wasn't going to tell a story, not about Hudson, or Balboa, or even about the woman who married him.

"Don't laugh," I told him, thinking that we both knew the rules.

Martha's Tomatoes

"But I, Sir Arthur, saw the Holy Grail,
I saw the Holy Grail and heard a cry—
O Galahad, and O Galahad, follow me."

—*Lord Tennyson*

Martha walked in front of me, her head straight and constant.

Green fields were separated by a gray slab of highway, and she turned back to see if I was behind her.

Martha had a passion for tomatoes, deeply red, sweet, and come July, in Iowa, she would initiate this journey to our neighbor's vegetable stand.

My sister turned back to me, but didn't say a word, and kept walking.

A semitrailer whined past, throwing dust and wind. I assumed that she brought me along, so I would not tell on her. My father had compared this road to an interstate, making it clear that we were not to walk beside it.

"What do you want, Snitch," she asked at the vegetable stand's counter.

She called me "Snitch," half little snot and half little witch, and people called her "the judge's daughter." That was a royal title, it seemed to me.

Our neighbor hailed his son from a tractor, a shirtless guy who was both wet and dusty. He helped Martha bag up her six tomatoes, putting them one by one into a crumpled sack. With each one, his eyes looked into the bag, then up to my sister. She looked around as if she might buy a cabbage.

She might buy a cabbage.

Martha was weird about food.

"Do you have to go right home," he asked.

Martha looked at me, then at him.

"Stay just a little while," he said.

He went around the counter, and they both began walking away from me, and while Martha never said anything, I knew I'd better not follow them.

I went and sat underneath a willow tree, and to pass the time, imagined that I was sitting underneath a head of hair.

Martha stood behind a tractor wheel, and the neighbor's son was in front of her in the same space.

Marie Antoinette's, I thought.

I turned to Martha, and she had her arms around the guy's neck.

A great rumble and roar was heard on the streets. The Parisian mob was marching to the palace.

Then there was the sound of a car door. I looked up and was now facing my father, a glaring white shirt, as if cut in half by his tie.

I thought about Martha.

"Tomatoes," I said.

He just stood there, then pointed to the car. "I have to be in court in five minutes."

It was going to be a long ride to the courthouse, and I lifted myself from the grass, making sure that I didn't look over at my sister.

The courthouse was red brick and old with two square towers on either side of its roof.

My father turned the steering wheel with one hand, and we were in the back parking lot, and a block-like concrete staircase led to his office.

He opened the closet, and his robe hung from a hook on the oak door.

He put it on and then walked over to a built-in file cabinet on one wall.

"Here," he said. "Read this." He dropped a file in front of me and made an exit to the adjoining courtroom. My father had left me his judgment on a hit and run case, black and white photos of the victim.

I liked to sit in his chair, it was huge, dark red, leather on wheels.

A picture of Martha was on his desk, the judge's daughter, and I looked at his wall of files, wondering which one he would give her. Off with her head, I thought to myself, or maybe my father would just put her in the tower.

His chair could be a throne. I imagined it to be a throne, and a writ was in front of me, a king's royal decree, the law of the land.

I was now not a snitch, not a snot, but a knitch, a knight, and devoted to protecting the honor of the grumpy old maiden, and she would lead me to the grail, the cup, the chalice, still marked by the blood of Christ.

Galahad, Percivale, and Bors.

My horse now slipped, and I turned the chair sharply, then back again.

"Did you learn anything," my father asked. The door closed behind him.

He picked up the file, returning it, took off his robe, returning it also. He took his pen from his shirt, writing a date on a piece of paper.

"Yes," I told him.

"Let's go," he said. He shut off the lights, then turned back.

"Don't you want your tomatoes?"

Reading
Thoreau

Jay Anderson drove a 1962 Austin-Healy convertible, had gorgeous blue eyes, and for one whole summer was the guy I wanted to marry. I played the harmonica that summer and carried around a hardback of Henry David Thoreau. I read passages in the access lanes to cornfields. There was no better place to learn about nature, cultivated nature.

Fleshy green fields, on either side of us, in front of us.

Behind us was a blacktop road.

It seemed delightfully subversive to read to him. The long sentences were best, flowing clauses, seemingly never ending. He listened. His eyes listened. What magic. What utter magic to have captivated his mind in a car far too small to make love in.

My interest in him began at homecoming, a pregame party. He had drunk too much Jack Daniels and apple cider, and was left behind in a strange apartment. I sat beside him on the couch, holding an orange Tide bucket by his head. He gagged, coughed, clear stuff running from his mouth.

An older blond, maybe twenty-seven, walked in and out of the kitchen. She acted as if we were invisible. I took her coolness to mean, how disgusting. Isn't he a prize? Do you suppose he could go to the bathroom?

"I'm sick," he said.

"I know," I told him.

I stroked his hair, black beautiful hair, thinking that my willingness to stay with him through this helpless display was a true sign of commitment, even though Florence Nightingale was not a heroine in my mind: I hadn't finished her biography.

In March, I took Jay to a lecture by Angela Davis. I was into the counterculture. He listened to her with his eyes, and a huge black woman sat beside him.

"Ms. Davis is an intelligent woman, but I don't think she's a wise woman."

Jay discussed the qualities of the speaker's mind with the professor, and that night, I read him Davis' address to the student body at Berkeley.

Was she intelligent? Was she wise?

In May, it was Stokely Carmichael. Jay's willingness to attend the symposium assured me that he was not the typical son of a paint manufacturer. He was undaunted by the former Black Panther's Marxist theme: "Where there is oppression, there is also resistance." The talk discussed rightful ownership of the products of labor, with a passionate rebuke of the bourgeoisie, and its violent theme frightened me.

"Scary, huh?"

"Why?" Jay asked earnestly.

At a park, atop a steel-beamed sculpture that gave one the impression of surveying the downtown from a Ferris wheel, I told Jay about Gandhi, and about how a nation had freed itself of colonial rule by the widespread use of the spinning wheel. I told him about the march to the sea, symbolizing India's attempt to reclaim independence through economic control of salt. He ran his hand across my back, undoing my bra. Gandhi's call for peaceful resistance had transcended worldly strife like hunger and physical bondage.

I moved down to a lower beam. A streetlight lit one corner of the pavement in front of Gabe and Walker's, making my new vantage point seem like a balcony, where below, some act may begin or had just ended. My bra rattled against my skin, as if noise had suddenly become tactile. Jay stepped down beside me on the rail. I turned my back to him, smiled. "Fix it. Let's go back."

"Can I stay over?"

"Yes," I told him.

Of course, I couldn't marry him, really marry him without meeting his mother. It was decided that I would meet her alone: She wanted to discuss "womanly" things. So in preparation for this event, I tried to remember the names of flowers. Flowers seemed womanly to me. My mother and grandmother grew them and, more so, knew their names.

Jay's mother sat on an ottoman, looking at me. Pictures of Jay were on the wall, at every age, and in every kind of costume: a cub scout, a cowboy, a blooming socialite clad in a white shirt with cuff links.

"You're Laura," she said.

I smiled, waiting for her to say something else. Now I noticed the paint cans, a row of paint cans lined the room. Some of the cans were old, with dripped dry paint, white, mostly white, and the trail became a stack.

"I understand that my son wants to marry you."

"Jay and I really get along," I said. I smiled. "He's great." She snorted.

"I love Jay." I picked up a magazine. What was I doing? I put it down.

"You're left-handed." Her observation startled me. "And it also seems that you're right-eyed. Mixed-handedness," she

Myrtle Hedge Press is pleased to provide your department/library with a review copy of feminist author Mattie McClane's *Unbuttoning Light*. Enjoy the book and consider keeping this book and other Mattie McClane titles in your collection. Order today!

muttered as if to herself. "I've done research on children with learning disabilities."

"That's interesting," I said.

She walked over to a huge desk, opened a drawer. Jay's mother rolled a piece of paper into a funnel. "Would you mind looking into this cone for me?"

"I suppose not."

"You're right-eyed, right-eyed and left-handed." She smoothed the paper into her hand, stroking it, thinking about the results of her test.

"How many children are in your family?"

"Three."

Your father, what's he do for a living? Will he ever return to private practice? I just kept answering her questions. How did I arrive at this university? What was my family's health history?

Did I have braces on my teeth as a child. She had belonged to the La Leche League.

"Do you intend to breast-feed?"

No wedding, no honeymoon, no moment of conception, no grueling childbirth experience, and the woman wanted to know the plans for my breasts.

"Well, Laura, let me tell you about boys like Jay." She looked me in the eyes. She paused. "He's had a privileged life, and I'm sure that must seem attractive to you. But boys like him are behind the others; they're slow to mature. Jay's too young for marriage."

I squirmed. My hand dropped to my chest, and I quickly moved it away. "Thank you," I said, just wanting to get away from her, her pictures, and all her cans.

"I'm sorry."

"Don't be sorry," I said.

Jay pulled up to the curb. Flashing his teethy perfect smile.

"How'd it go?"

"Not good," I told him.

I didn't say anything so Jay began to drive. He was heading for the cornfields, somewhere to talk. Finally the car stopped. There was silence, dead, still silence. Clouds seemed to leak white onto a baby blue background, and I refused to look at his wonderful eyes.

"How about some Thoreau?"

Okay. I leafed through the pages of Walden Pond, and began a monotonous drone, listening to the sound of lengthy sentences, thinking about landscape: There was something transcendent about cornfields; one's mind couldn't dwell on them for long, unlike mountains that inspire awe of their own beauty, and they weren't vast or mysterious like oceans, and were easy to forget, even as one looked at them, no aspects or particulars, just land melding green.

I looked up and sought out a husk of corn. Jay moved close to me and rested his head against my blouse. I pretended to adjust myself in the car's seat, gently directing him away from me, alltogether certain that if I could read slowly and long enough, he would simply fall asleep.

Naming
Charlie

"What's wrong, little chicken?"

"This isn't fun, Charlie." My skis acted like the hard remains of a banana, going this way, and then that way, and white was the only color on the mountain, covering boulders, masking ledges. My cheeks were cold, and I imagined that my face was red, a contrast to the snow.

Ice crystals formed on Charlie's mustache like road salt, and he stood straight, easy, on the slope.

"Charlie leaves me here and catches up with the others. I go up the hill and slide down, and I think I've done that ten times. :

"Why don't I just meet you guys at the car?"

"It's your wax, just let me put some wax on your skis," he said mournfully.

Charlie turned his head, looked upward towards the summit, the direction of his friends. "Come on, be a bull chicken." A chicken was just a chicken, but a bull chicken could keep up with a band of his friends.

Charlie stabbed the tip of his ski pole into the snow.

"Okay then."

I put my arm behind me and tried to lift myself. "I'll go down with you, but let me go up and tell them that we're going to the bar; otherwise, they'll wonder about us."

Charlie pushed off with his poles and walked up the mountainside. He turned back to me.

"Don't go anywhere."

I imagined his friends and knew that they wouldn't wonder about us.

Charlie and I, on these weekends, back from the bar, back to the condo, disappeared into a bedroom. We'd leave them, and their conversations about the necessity of carrying extra ski tips, green wax.

They'd cook spaghetti and bought gallon bottles of red wine and raisins.

Raisins. They'd ski ten miles around a mountain and then stop to eat raisins: It was a ritual and the raisins were part of it.

Why raisins, Charlie, I wanted to asked but never did. He would not speculate about dried grapes.

Johann Svee, I named him that.

He named me, my moods, my facial expressions.

I liked nouns, proper nouns, people found in history, types, and he applied adjectives to nouns, and that was kinder, more flexible; after all, to name something was to claim understanding.

I named all sorts of people, though, not just Charlie. A reclusive woman lived across from my apartment, and seeing only her trash, bagged and bundled, ad if it were going away to camp, I named her Emily, for Emily Dickinson, and she probably didn't write poetry. But it's hard to wonder about a person without a name.

I could have named her Greta, after the Swedish film star, who said she wanted to be alone, or Baby Doe, the wife of the silver king, Horace; after he lost his fortune and died, she became a recluse in Leadville, lived in a shack, and went it alone. Horace had her portrait painted on a barroom floor, the stuff of legend and mining lore.

I wondered if Horace named her Baby Doe. Her mother didn't. A woman wouldn't name a daughter after a female deer; it was an endearment or maybe a name she gave to herself. A pioneer woman might name herself, on the edge of a wilderness, surrounded by uncertainty.

She might name herself. Adeline Virginia Stephen became just Virginia Woolf. George Duckworth called her "Goat," and Kathleen Beauchamp took her grandmother's maiden name and renamed herself Katherine Mansfield. Her husband called her "Tig," short for tiger.

Baby Doe didn't name herself. Horace named her, I thought.

I watched Charlie fasten skis to a metal rack on the top of his jeep.

At the bottom of Berthoud Pass was a bar, usually empty, with rusty kettles and lanterns, mountain artifacts, hung along the walls. It was a meeting place for miners who worked at the Henderson.

It was between shifts, and now rows of denim and checkered shirts lined the counter.

Charlie looked at me. "What do you want?" he asked, and then walked to the side of the bar.

His orange gaiters contrasted with the heavy black boots between the legs of barstools, and he looked out of place, as if he had just been cut out of a ski catalog and pasted to this setting.

A woman was talking to him from where she sat, and her voice was loud.

Her voice rang out in all directions, to different men along the row.

Charlie said something to her, turned back and looked at me, and now his eyes were fixed downward, and his hand lifted the dollars on the bar nervously, playing with them, picking them up, letting them fall.

Charlie smiled. Her voice became louder, and it was as if a light were on him, and every head turned his way, but I could not hear what was going on, just the woman bantering, talking.

Charlie returned to the table with our drinks, set them down, spilling a little of one.

"She's just drunk."

"Do you want to leave?"

"Maybe," Charlie said.

The room was too quiet and the miners talked between themselves, occasionally looking over at us. "Let's wait a minute," he said.

Finally he stood. I followed him. Just past the bar, the woman called out to him again.

He looked at her, and a man turned, hitting Charlie hard in the face.

I just stood there, waiting for him to take running steps backwards, as if he were caught in a horrible wind, and it was blowing him back. His arms would be out, as if he were trying to catch himself on something solid, finding only air, and then he would crash into a counter or a window, and that would be it.

Or he would block an approaching swing, arms crossed, for a second, and then release a counterpunch, knocking the bad guy down. I had never seen anyone hit in the face, and it amazed me how undramatic violence was in reality, it was deadening, film rolling in slow motion.

A barstool toppled to one of its legs, seemed to twirl, like a dancer that bowed to the floor, and I waited for something to happen, a next move.

But there wasn't one, just long stares. Charlie set the glass that he was still holding on the bar. Then he turned. "Let's go," he said.

"Didn't you want to hit him?" I asked. I held a washcloth to his chin, sat on a bed, and put on his shirt so I could go to the sink at the end of the hall.

"Scrappy chicken," he said.

"Rub my back."

Charlie sat on my butt.

"Not at all, Charlie?"

"Not until I left."

One of his friends slapped the door on the way to the bathroom.

I could smell oregano and feel Charlie on my back, lying down on me, and he was not a type from stories, not a recluse, not a hero from a motion picture, and not a silver king, just Johann Svee: I had found name without history.

West of the Pecos

D ave and I sat on a tweed couch, in his apartment, with the television on, some western movie on the screen, and we seemed to be watching it.

I had brought a bill over for him to look at, for his opinion on. He was an attorney, a guy whom I dated in college: Our arguments were legendary.

I didn't feel like fighting, actually I felt as if a huge rock had hit me on the head, and I was stunned, maybe dead. The bill that I brought Dave invalidated 10,000 signatures, and two years of my work in managing a campaign for county consolidation in Iowa.

In a meeting with the house majority leader, I had been advised to "get on with something else." I remember smiling, telling him that wasn't possible. He answered me with a new filing date, and according to the law, my petitions were three weeks late, and so, no good.

Dave rubbed his eye. "I don't know what to tell you." A posse stopped at the top of a sandy hill, the riders waving their guns.

He looked over to me, but I didn't turn my face away from the movie. The helpless woman, I thought, and it was probably okay to cry in front of him, certainly I had before, but he couldn't do anything to change this situation. "The wording is black and white," Dave added.

"It was targeted at my effort."

"You can't prove that, Laura."

I watched the heroine extend her arms to a man wearing a dark shirt and imagined that he dropped her, but, of course, he did a one-handed lift, and they rode away. The next scene had to be at a hideout, and a handsome outlaw would be wounded, bleeding in a bedroom.

"What do you think you can do?"

I smiled, wickedly, shook my head, and while my campaign might have been the issue, the source of anger, it was more than that too. "I have to go," I said. I heard my words, the old script, but now he didn't stand in front of me, bend down, talk into my face.

⌒

The judge read the bill, and it was strange to have my father at the kitchen table without it being a holiday. "What did Dave Telleen say?"

"He thought it was black and white, no recourse, not a lot to do."

My father stood, paced along the counter, holding his fedora. He stopped, and began tapping his hat on the breadbox. Here it comes, I thought, a lecture on not watching legislation in the middle of a drive. "You're going to file the petitions anyway," he said.

"If you don't file them, you can't test the law in the courts, can you?"

"I want you to hold a series of press conferences.Say first that you're thinking of filing the petitions; next, that you've decided to, and then that you're thinking of a suit …. Your buddies in Des Moines don't want a spotlight."

"Drag it out."

"But," he continued, "Whatever you say, you must do."

The judge shook his head, looking at the floor. "It's illegal to file a lawsuit for the sake of publicity, and especially if you have no case. And you have no case that I can see except that their move was intentional."

"They've thrown you a hardball, have tried to knock you down. I want you to throw it back to them just as hard, and put them on their asses."

I stroked my eyebrow, not looking at him, and he sensed my defeat. It angered him.

"Look," he said. "Nobody in this business has to like you. But you're not going to last long if they don't respect you."

My father now seemed like a character in a western movie, Roy Bean, Justice of the Peace, the law west of the Pecos, and I was some lone woman.

Phoebe Ann Moses, a.k.a. Annie Oakley, sharpshooter, born in 1860 in Ohio, took her first shot at age eight, followed a circuit of road shows, married Frank Butler. born in 1860 in Ohio.

"Okay," I said. "I know." Tomorrow I'd visit the editor of the newspaper, release the news, respond to it. I'd tell him that I intended litigation.

~

In a conference room, Dan Hanson sat on a black leather sofa, with his arm stretched out along the top of it, as if he had it around a girlfriend, he picked at its fabric, smiling, as if he were waiting for me to tell him something he didn't know, anything.

I suggested that the county campaign had been killed by its opponents.

The house majority leader had managed the legislation, tacked a new deadline onto an appropriations bill. I told him about my meeting with Roberts, about his feeling that any attempt to consolidate counties would damage his party's organization: Counties were building blocks for money and volunteers.

Hanson stood, walked to the door, leaving me silent, and he motioned unto the newsroom, returning to his seat; a reporter joined us.

"My only recourse is to file the petitions, and test the law in the courts."

"10,000 signatures seemed like enough of a mandate to do so." My steady voice pleased me.

"Nothing more simple, I assure you. But I'll tell you what. You must have your mind, your nerve, and everything in harmony. Don't look at your gun, simply follow the object with the end of it, as if the tip of the barrel was the tip of your finger."

—Annie Oakley

I planned press conferences, held them on the capitol steps. Reporters investigated, and more information came to light on just who had initiated the quashing deadline, and the press began to wonder about Roberts' rationale for changing the procedural statute.

My father said, "More light. Nothing scares the guilty like inquiry."

I began to sense that I was going to win, that the workings of a legislature could be called to turn if one of its powerful members were in trouble. I received a phone call from the deputy attorney general, and he asked me to submit my grievance to his office.

I told him I'd think about it.

"Don't even think about it," my father screamed into the telephone.

I called every attorney friend. I called every friend who knew an attorney. I'd like to help, but you have no case, I was told, or that I couldn't expect so much from Democratic law firms. Dave gave me the name of a woman who was in practice with a manic depressive, struggling to pay her rent. The manic depressive wasn't the one he recommended, but, I assumed, was mentioned to make the one I might hire sound as odd as possible. She agreed and prepared a writ of mandamus.

The next headline ran: Lawsuit Expected over County Ballot.

⌒

He was a long, tall Texan, and behind him was the light of the sun, and it was morning, and the sky was cloudless, and his white horse clawed the sand.

My dress was thin and cotton, pale, maybe soft, conforming to the wind, hot or cold, day or night, and my hair blew across my breasts.

"What are you doing?"

"What do you mean?"

"A judge will throw it out."

"Thank you, Dave."

"I'm not being cruel," he said. "I don't want to see you get hurt."

But Mr. Telleen, I imagined myself saying, I am left out all alone on this desert, and at night the coyotes whine, the air's cold, and I've already walked a very long way; there's something like blood on my face, and you are looking at me, why can't you see it?

⌒

A state representative from Johnson County called me, and suggested that the legislature could vote to put the county consolidation question on the ballot. He'd be willing to sponsor the resolution if I liked.

"That's it. It's over," my father said. "Call him back and tell him you'd very much like that, the bastard."

Phone calls from reporters woke me up the next morning, at seven thirty. Yes, I felt the legislature made an honorable move; it was not expected, yes, and I was pleased.

"Are you basking in credibility, Laura?"

"A pretty amazing turn, Charlie." I was beside my husband, not really thinking, but tired of thinking, about trust, about doubt, about Mr. Telleen.

Unbuttoning
Light

"Charlie?"

"I'm listening."

I sat in front of a seventh-floor hotel window, in the dark, in my slip, holding a water glass of champagne. The blue light of a squad car spun around the downtown buildings. Orange neon outlined the words, "Chicago's finest."

"My mother seemed like an avenging angel that day. She had on this winter white suit, her eyes were green and wet like the inside of a grape. But she couldn't stay mad, Charlie. She didn't take me out of that place. They just decided that I wasn't contagious."

"Charlie?"

"I'm still listening."

Taillights, headlights alternated red and white on the street below. The window framed my view of the outside world and held together bits of disjointed scenes, half stories, parts of sentences, paragraphs bursting with sensuous light, streaming with emotion so untold.

Charlie sat up in the bed behind me.

"Why tonight? We go to Dave's wedding, drive into the city, and then all of this. Church. Bitchy nuns. Forgive me, dear, but it's almost two in the morning. What's the connection? What's got you going on this?"

"I don't know." I did know or was closer to knowing than I was willing to let on. The jagged pieces were lining up, beginning to form a picture. Year-round Christmas lights twinkled from a pawnbroker's window on the next block, red, green, blue, and if only in the dark, I was fond of my white half-nakedness. I decided to let Charlie sleep. The day tumbled with a part of the past, fired, shone, began taking form.

I thought my new suit might save me. I looked at its white buttons and thought how carefully I had chosen it, standing at the mirror, thinking nothing sleazy, nothing red, and certainly nothing white.

It was the perfect pose and teal, something in Nancy Reagan's closet, affecting that all the passions in the world were put on for a camera, so young, so intelligent, so civic-minded: It couldn't possibly let on that I felt as if I might die. The buttons, though, were the best.

My husband handed me an umbrella.

Rain hurled like shot against the windshield, and the car's wipers beat it back. The clouds were gray, moving across the sky, mixing, hanging, almost vertically.

"What a day for a wedding." Charlie looked to me. I didn't reply. His hand was on the boot just below the transmission stick, and he put the car into reverse.

"So what's Cathy's maiden name?" He laughed. "Catherine Smiddle or Diddle?"

"Catherine Smiddle or Diddle Telleen?" Charlie wanted me to join in his playfulness.

"It's on the invitation," I said, but made no effort to retrieve the card from the glove compartment.

"Do you know what she does?"

She irons shirts, makes dip out of Velveeta, cans green beans, plays cribbage, cheats at hearts, doesn't play Scrabble, buys inflated bras, has a surprised look on her face, reads women's magazines.

"Charlie, I don't know much about her."

I watched familiar buildings pass by, a school, a dentist's office with its sign missing a vowel. What difference did it make about a name, Tim or Tom, Smiddle or Diddle? My new suit wasn't working.

"Charlie Parks," a tall usher put his hand out to my husband.

"The bride or the groom?"

"The groom. Actually he's an old friend of my wife's. They did their college internships together in Washington, D.C., worked for the same senator."

I listened to Charlie give the explanation, wondered why he was so matter-of-fact. But his version of the story was comforting, a stating of facts, simple and true, as they were reported to him though lacking.

I felt hands on my shoulders. I turned, facing Rich, another intern who had been with us that year. "Laura." He gave me a hug.

"It's good to see you. I wasn't sure if you'd make it." His eyes looked sad, too sympathetic.

It was one thing to be here and quite another for someone else to know that I didn't want to be. I rubbed my suit button like it either had to be a charm or would, at once, become a point of access to what was underneath and allow my guts to rush out onto the floor.

"How could I miss Dave's wedding?"

I booked airline tickets to New York, cancelled them. I invited an out-of-town friend for the weekend: She couldn't make it. I invented sick children, very sick children with droopy eyelids, raging fevers.

The usher took me by the arm.

A nun led me by the top of my shirt sleeve into the hall. Her eyes looked like brown beans, hard and woody, extending far back into her head. I thought that she might spin if she let go of me, convulse into a wobbly orbit.

"Stay here," she said.

At the end of the corridor was an arched stained-glass window showing Jesus healing lepers, and these figures, sick and unliked, knelt beside him. The light shifted, cut across colored bits and rested on his face. I looked at his face, the afternoon sunlight. I heard nuns' voices, their square heels clicking on the floor.

The two women were now beside me, viewing me, a second grader in their school.

"She still has the chicken pox."

The principal put her hand underneath my chin, raised it, lifted it, until I was looking directly at her, and our eyes were in alignment.

"Are you sick, Laura?"

"No," I told her, wanting to take my head off her hand, imagining the movement. I could edge it off slowly or jerk it away, and it seemed that these were my choices. But instead I stood perfectly still and decided not to see her.

"She most certainly is sick." The other nun pulled up my blouse from the navy-blue skirt, causing a button to tear away. "You can still see the marks, and it's beyond me why her mother would send her to school."

The two women talked between themselves, and their heads jiggled from their conversation. I then turned my thoughts to the stained glass window, wishing for a miracle, not for unblemished skin and divine healing. I simply prayed that the sky would split open and a force remove me.

Ushers rolled out a carpet. Music played. Dave took his place at the altar. In a few minutes, I predicted, the bride would enter.

Charlie put his hand on mine.

I thought about waffle irons, and wondered if anybody ever purchased them except for wedding gifts. What was the point of a machine that made patterned pancakes and ended up in the cupboard above the refrigerator? I tried to imagine an urgency for such an item.

I thought about Maine, about honeymoons.

Rich turned back from a pew in front of me and smiled. I smiled also, unsure that I could go through with this now. I planned to imagine the bride as a great white goose, awkward, nervous, mostly surprised to be in a church.

The priest chanted in Latin, and it meant nothing to me in the second grade. His strange sentences set my mind dreaming, thinking about pictures, windows, the small shapes, that in their union formed stories.

"You fidget."

"You won't sit still."

"I'll call your mother," the nun told me as a threat, like there was a real chance that my mother was meaner than she. The outside sunlight swayed across the colored panels, and in that same light the dove's eyes twinkled, and the thin arms of Jesus Christ glistened in the heat.

Charlie put his arm around me, listening to the Gospel According to St. John: "… the ruler of the feast had tasted the wine and knew not whence it was: the governor of the feast called the bridegroom."

And saith unto him, every good man at the beginning doth set forth good wine and when men have well drunk, then that which is worse: but thou hast kept the good until now."

I wondered about this miracle and how many times I heard about Christ turning water into wine. It seemed that, in his goodness, in his infinite divine goodness, he might also turn wine back into water.

"Laura?"

"Yes, Charlie."

"Are you coming to bed?"

"Yes, Charlie."

Amends

"You think it's stupid."

"It's your body. I'm not going to tell you what to do with it," I said as if it were the first time that we had discussed the breast implants, and now, actually sitting in the lobby of a boob job specialist, a certified plastic surgeon, it seemed a little late to offer pros and cons, as though the decision had not been made.

Martha turned her face away.

"It'll be good for my marriage."

I looked at her, then looked away.

I decided that I would stay with Martha until she went under, return to the lobby, read magazines, art reviews, world reports.

I would catch up on the latest tabloid gossip, Princess Di and Charles quarrel, that kind of stuff. I would learn the twenty-five secrets to better sex, how to hang on to your man, glamour tips.

I would fill out a quiz on my personality, my marriage, my sex drive.

I would not watch the surgeon scrape tissue and reshape my sister's breasts.

Yesterday, in his office, he took a pen and drew the procedure on a sheet of paper, circles within circles, configurations that looked like fried eggs. Posters were on the wall, women displaying the range of possibilities, B to D cups, the success stories, before and after.

An editor once told me that she returns stamped postcards from lawn care companies with a message of her own: Why don't you guys get into a legitimate business? The chemicals you use mess up the river? I watched his pen indicate areas that would be removed and words akin to "quack" ran through my mind, a specialist boob, the best in Illinois.

Tarbell, Ida. American author, muckraker, informed citizens about abuses of power at Standard Oil. Born in Erie County, Pennsylvania, studied in Paris, magazine editor.

Joseph Lister, professor of surgery at Edinburgh from 1869 to 1877. Lister insisted on the use of antiseptics on hands and instruments, and by doing so, made it safe for doctors to open abdomens, heads, or chests. Breasts.

Martha blushed and nodded. The doctor held the results from a mammogram; all systems were go. Now all she had to do was decide the size, and he urged her to take her time, not to act in haste, because often women regretted not going as large as possible, shyness, he supposed.

"How dangerous is this?" I asked. He looked at me, now sensing a rebel in the ranks. "I mean the surgery itself, and in the long-term?"

Andrew Jackson didn't consent to shine, boots of a British officer at Waxhaw, S.C., arguing that he had rights as a prisoner of war. The commander drew his sword, the boy put up his hands to defend himself, and his left was cut to the bone. His brother Robert stood by his side.

I had written about breast implants, the silicone kinds, the ones approved and later retrieved by the FDA in an article. How was it that I stood in a doctor's office pretending to comply with procedures that I had publically denounced? I thought about consistency, about Janus, two faces, one looking forward, the other looking back.

The god of gates, doors, passages. No I was not a rebel, no Jackson at Waxhaw. I simply had two faces and wasn't at all sure which was mine.

"Yes, of course, there's risk, risk in any surgery, but we've discussed that."

Martha seemed hurt by my question, like she still hadn't convinced me that this was for the best, another cat out of a bag, and I wondered why I never learned to be quiet when it was pointless to speak. The surgeon picked up his pen, put his telephone number on the top of the paper, and gave it to her. "If you get back to your hotel room and have questions or concerns, call me at home."

"Otherwise, I'll see you in the morning."

She never called him, and last night in our hotel room, I listened to stories about nervous romantic encounters, stories about being afraid to take a shower in gym class, about the paranoia of wearing a padded bra, about bold sales clerks and a dressing room nightmare.

"I called her a bitch."

"For walking in on you?" I remembered that day. How angry my mother was, pushing shopping bags onto the kitchen table. Martha was fifteen, and despite my mother's demand that Martha apologize to the girl, who was just doing her job, my sister refused, stood silently for twenty minutes.

"I would've been a different person if I would've had a normal breast size," she told me in the dark, the television screen still blue.

You would've been loose, I thought to myself and wondered if there wasn't an advantage in being repressed. Surely something came from our hang ups. I thought about my nose. It was probably a good thing that it was right there on my face and needed no unveiling.

Unbuttoning Light

Besides I was once told that smart people had large noses, important people, statesmen, presidents, writers, the thinking types. Having not thought about that for a long time, I wondered where one came up with such nonsense, and how inclined I had been to believe it.

The surgical assistant put clear tubes into Martha's nose. I noticed that she had freckles still.

Count to eleven, she counted to six, and was still. The doctor eyed me. Yes, I was leaving; do your thing, I thought. It wasn't his fault, no it wasn't his fault that my sister wouldn't say she was sorry to the shop girl, that she married a Neanderthal plumber, that my mother was built, or that I had so easily accepted the big nose theory of intelligence and not a more credible notion about big breasts.

That notion was at least logical, affirmed by magazines, films, boyfriends, passing glances, swimsuits. Only I believed in large noses, in pictures of Emerson and Roosevelt, silently, but maybe, yes, maybe.

Emerson had written about self-reliance, about manners, about history, friendship, love, culture, heroism, scholarship. He had written about civilization, the over-soul, great men, poets, mystics, generals, essay after essay, but had not one thought about noses or breasts.

"Don't forget your lunch."

"What lunch?" I asked Martha.

"Your lunch is on the counter."

The recovery room nurse smiled at me. "She'll be groggy for a while."

Martha smiled, then put her chin down, so she could better see the new vertical rise. I wanted to tell her that I was sorry for not wishing this for her, for fighting it, for not wanting to understand her stories about disappointed lovers and mirrors in the showers.

But I couldn't.

"Are they bigger," she asked.

"Big, Martha, they're big."

"Really?"

"Yes," I said.

Her head rested on the pillow, and she looked directly at me, so rare an exchange, that I wondered if her eye contact was because of the drugs, so steady, unflinching. Martha, I'm sorry, I said to myself.

My Mother's Voice

Mother knelt beside a Christmas tree, holding a porcelain angel in her hand.

Michael, Gabriel, the names of angels, the only names of angels that I knew, I thought.

St. Raphael.

Mother didn't see me, and so I watched her untangle a blue thread from the figure's arm, turning the string, and then the angel. She smoothed its hair, putting the strands between two fingers, and held it up as if she were checking its overall appearance.

She placed it on the tree.

Angelos in Greek, spiritual messengers who stood in foaming clouds.

Angels, archangels, the nine choirs of angels, cherubim and seraphim, powers, virtues, dominions, and thrones, the hierarchy of heaven.

Some angels were more powerful than others, and I wondered why.

Mother had caught an unsure glimpse of me; she turned slightly, and then more fully, but her facial expression looked like she had been caught.

"Come on in, Laura," she said.

I stood in the hallway between the kitchen and the foyer with my stomach jutting out from my coat. My coat was blue and wool: It could no longer be buttoned on account of my being eight months pregnant.

I had just had a negative sonogram for twins, just a big baby, maybe ten pounds.

My mother must have thought that I looked tired, so she moved a chair closer to me.

"Are you feeling okay?" she asked.

"Not really," I told her. "I chaired a public hearing today, and this lady told me that I looked like an elephant. Imagine running a meeting, in front of television crews, after that news." I stretched out my leg, gently touching the end of a tree branch with the tip of my shoe. Mother's angels began to sway.

"After that, I could have been Dumbo," I said. I thought about the metaphor, Dumbo was Walt Disney, Jumbo was P.T. Barnum. Dumbo was a cartoon character. Jumbo was an attraction in a travelling show.

Jumbo, the giant elephant purchased from a London zoo, added a new word to the English language to describe bigness and joined Barnum's show in 1883.

Dumbo who needed a feather to fly, was the hero in a children's tale about the power of illusion in prompting courage.

"I do think you're trying to do too much now," my mother said finally.

She paused.

"You know, I wasn't able to perform then." I predicted that she was going to tell me how she quit singing after Martha was born.

It was just too much, and about how my father was jealous of the attention she received from other men, and how she had just given it up.

I looked at her angel collection, the solid china faces and unbending pleated gowns.

Hark, the herald angels sing. She sings like an angel. The choir of angels.

I looked at my mother and then once more at her favorite ornaments.

Lind, Jennie (1820-1887), a soprano whose vocal control won her the title of "The Swedish Nightingale," had a brilliant career in opera and on the concert stage. She joined P.T. Barnum's circus after 1849, touring the United States.

I looked at the tree branches, one rising above the other, angels leveled and rising to the top, towards the star, like a hierarchy of heaven, and each figure had its place. I wondered what happened to angels who, suddenly, one day, woke up without a voice, their messages muted, silent. For if, in heaven, there was a hierarchy for angels, it had something to do with the power in one's voice.

"Sing, Mother," I said.

She turned. "What?"

"Sing something, anything."

She smiled, like she was thinking about it, like she might do it.

Then she shook her head.

"No," she said, "not now."

I watched her hands place another angel, a delicate and fine movement, and it seemed to me then, that I had imagined my mother, and who she was, not by her words, but by watching her, her movement.

I knew her understanding of light and shadows, of color and form, and by this muted understanding I knew her private soul.

I could see it and feel it as my own, but I could not approach her silence.

My baby rolled underneath my ribcage. I could hear my father in the dining room, his ritual of dumping files on the buffet upon returning home from the office. I could hear his wingtips on the ceramic floor.

Barnum, Phineas T. (1810-1891), who organized "The Greatest Show on Earth," was responsible for some of the greatest attractions of his time; he developed a method of promotion known as the "ballyhoo," a way of making known quickly a product of personality.

I heard his voice, "Geez, Laura, do you suppose you can get any bigger?" He laughed. I imagined a tattooed caller behind a ticket booth.

See General Tom Thumb, elephants Jumbo and Toung Taloung, the original white elephant, the nurse of George Washington. See an angel who does not sing.

Young and Early Stories

Recreating
Jeopardy

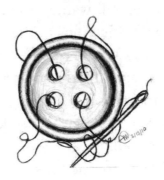

Sports

Kate pulled her chin up onto his chest, moved it in circles as if she were drawing with it, careful, exacting. Jack's gaze was fixed on the ceiling. "Wake up, Jack Ivanovich," she said to redirect his attention. He groaned. Still his eyes appeared to scrutinize the overhead light. She brought a sheet up across his stomach. He stared. Kate straightened it. He ignored her.

"Let's play a game, Jack. It's called 'what are you thinking right now?'" He looked to her. "It's my game so let's divide the possible answer into categories." Jack smiled. "How about sports, world peace, doctors, and knicks and knacks?" He rolled to his side and propped his head with the palm of his hand.

"I'll try world peace," she said as she looked his way once more to see if he still wanted to play. "I bet you are thinking about the ramifications of the Geneva Summit?" He grinned. "No, no, I know, you are thinking that polo really is a dangerous game?" Jack's smile was full, open now. "No, that's not it. You are thinking that the only reason I sleep with you is because you have eyes like a revolutionary, like Lenin's." He frowned.

"Ohhh, Katie." Jack dropped his head to the mattress. "Vladimir Ilyich Ulyanov, huh? Actually I am thinking how spoiled you are. You want it both ways. You're happy with this arrangement."

Kate knew that the fun was over. He was going to start. She watched him stand. His legs were long and skinny. "It's time to go home, Katie," his voice projected for effect. "Your hubby awaits. Who does he have eyes like?"

⌒

One leg went into his trousers, then the other. "You're making this a sleazy deal," he said louder. A green-patterned tie was in his hands. Shades of green went through her mind, fir green, moss green, jade green, emerald green.

Jack bent down to her. He said softly as if between his teeth, "I can't stand this anymore. Do you hear me? Make a decision." Jack took his coat from the back of a chair and walked to the door, then turned to her. The door slammed.

He left without a sock. It was on the floor like a sleeping kitten. Kate imagined his one bony ankle exposed to the cab driver. The thought amused her. Jack amused her, his dramatic exits. She would not make a decision. He knew it too.

Kate pulled a robe from the closet and walked to the window. Three men were replacing the sidewalk below and stood in a huddle, pointing here and there. A round man with a red cap stomped his foot on the pavement. Another man squared his face in front of the others and shook his head. Men argued about concrete! The round man threw up his hands. It now was resolved. They began removing equipment from the truck. The round man now smiled. Perhaps his antics paid off, his persuasion. He didn't look very persuasive to her; he looked silly.

Kate stomped her foot on the carpet. Dumb. Why did people think that control was gained by gestures? Why did everyone want to tell others what to do? Kate flipped Jack's sock over her shoulder. She decided to take a shower. The water was cold. It was time to go home.

⌒

The airport fluttered, shook like a wet bird. A family was burdened by skis. A mother chased a toddler around luggage, arranged like blocks, in tiers. Then there were the wanderers, the business crowd who pulled their possessions around on stainless carts. Kate checked the time. She expected to be home in two hours.

She watched her husband maneuver the side streets, the winding lanes. It was like a maze, the route to her house. The neighborhood smelled like nitrogen, potassium, the first application of lawn care. The junipers had been pruned to look oriental, the houses painted to look Swiss. Scotty remarked about rack and pinion steering, German engineering.

Kate stared out the car window. She could see her image in the glass, cast in faint tints, a spectrum, red to violet. Angles of white light shown on her lips, thin lines amidst distortion. Scotty said that she had missed a barbeque. She nodded with the hope that this gesture would cover anything she hadn't heard. "How's the book coming along? Are there problems with it? Seems like you've been working on it for a long time." Scotty looked to her.

"No, the book is fine. Jack Cassel knows Soviet politics. Details, I guess. Little things. "That's pretty much the delay." A child's lost kite twirled around a utility wire.

"It's not a big contract, not like a general requirements textbook. But he's credible, not a closet scholar. That appeals to me."

"So what's he like?" Scotty looked to her. "I mean what's a guy like who has spent the last two years in Russia? Sounds kind of gray."

Gray, yes gray, as opposed to horizon gold. The neighbors were painting their house. A scaffold hung below their bedroom window.

"He's just a professor, kind of awkward really."

The neighbors waved. The concept of guilt crossed her mind. It was in order. The car stopped. Her husband waggled the luggage to the front step. "It was a nice trip," she said to the people next door.

⌒

The oven door slammed. Frozen, stuffed bell peppers waited on the counter. She should feel something. Why couldn't she feel anything? Heat. Kate imagined the scenario, all the tension that proceeds an admission of wrong-doing. Scotty would be reading a magazine, a glossy pictorial account of European culture. Just as she began to discuss her infidelity, Scotty would recite capital cities, Berlin, Prague, Bern, Bucharest, Paris, London, Vienna … Did she know anymore? Did she have something on her mind?

Scotty paced about the kitchen, picking and poking through drawers of utensils, tongs. Kate leaned up against the cabinets as if the floor would, at any minute, begin to shake. Scotty wanted to start a flower garden. He wanted her to travel less. They should have a baby soon. The oven should be hot enough. Use the potholders. Go off the pill. Where were the oven mitts? He wanted the oven mitts. She didn't have to work. After the Soviet book, she could give notice. She could join the club. It would be fun, have a baby.

Kate walked to the window. Clouds swirled like milk poured into a glass of water, into and around the moon. The wind rushed them, pushed them in circles, then away from light and into darkness. Scotty continued.

The concept of guilt crossed her mind. Her chin was on his chest. Polo was a dangerous game. The sock was on her shoulder. Dark eyes were on her. It was a sport. Make a decision. Make a decision. She looked at Scotty, his eyes. Swatches of blue went through her mind, powder blue, royal blue, navy blue, azure. Kate turned to the cupboard where they kept their plates. "I am going to see Jack Cassel next week. Hopefully we can finish up with the book. But, Scotty, … I'm not going to make a decision about my job." Kate set the plates on the counter. "That's too much to ask," she said as she swept bread crumbs into her hand.

The days were getting longer. In the afternoon, she read contracts and manuscripts. She watched the neighbor's house being painted. The painter's over-sized shirt flapped in the breeze. Jack's manuscript was in order, ready for production. She had to send it on. His contract was in her hand, his named typed out in full, his signature. Scotty waved to her from the lawn tractor. Only two more days.

Balloons bobbed in the air. Children bawled. The downtown workers weaved around the shoppers. The sun lit the morning, an effective brilliance, stunning, energizing. Now Kate moved quickly through the crowd, noticing obstacles, faceless shapes, outlining a direction of movement. She looked for Jack and only for Jack. She imagined her arms around his neck, stretched against him in an open light. Children laughed. She could see the brownstone. Light sliced between the buildings, sharp and silver. She ran up the steps. The key. She put the key into the lock.

The door was jam

med. The lock was jammed. Kate tried again. She pulled the key out and stared at it. She tried the key again. The key would not turn the lock. She knocked on the door. Again. Harder. She fit the key into the lock. She slammed her hand up against the door.

A strange, crooked woman looked up at her from the bottom of the stairs. "He moved," she said. "The lease wasn't renewed."

World Peace

Scotty turned the front wheel, watched it spin, crooked, out of balance. A spoke was broken. Tools were all around him. The bicycle was parked in one corner of the kitchen. He knelt beside it as if he were playing a harp; thin canvass gloves were on his hands.

Kate stood at the sink. Mitchell played on the floor and had become interested in hiding his plastic key ring under the rug. He flipped the braided weave back and forth, revealing and concealing the molded colors. Out the window, Kate could see the postman making his rounds. It was springtime, though the air was quite warm. She watched the jeep pull in front of each house on the circle.

"I'm sorry, Scotty. But I can't imagine it," she said as the mail truck turned off into another part of the subdivision. He paid no apparent attention to her and kept spinning the broken wheel."

Then finally he asked her, "What's surgery here or surgery abroad?"

"Nobody's talking Vienna," Kate came back quickly.

"No, what's surgery here or surgery abroad? The facilities will be lesser," Scotty answered his own question. Look how one broken spoke messed up the whole action. It was amazing really. He brushed his hand across his forehead as if he were straightening his hair. There was a smear of bearing grease between his eyebrows.

Scotty looked up. "It's good for business. Dewey thinks so," he said as if a second opinion would sway the argument.

"It's a chance to do something good." He paused. "You know, the days of everyone out for themselves are over."

"Whatever happened to standing by at the high school football games? That's community service too." She watched him turn a screw.

"Scotty you can't really believe that the only difference between working here and working in Bosnia will be the facilities? Not you, nor Dewey White, nor Arlette, have any idea about a war zone."

"Katie, Katie, Katie." He stood, holding the frame of the bicycle in his hands. "What can I do to make you feel better on this?" Scotty shook his head. "The problem is that you're not a surgeon … It doesn't matter to me how a patient becomes injured." He set the bike down, putting his arm out to her. "You have read too many books, worked with too many know-it-alls … War is romantic and sentimental, sad or something." His eyes kept a steady gaze on the broken wheel. He lowered his voice. "Those are not my concerns."

The Whites' car could be heard in the driveway. Katie and Scotty exchanged a glance: the conversation would have to be put off until another time. Katie could tell that their arrival had put her husband at ease. He now examined the wheel as if a malfunction had just been discovered, intently and without distraction. They both waited for their friends to knock on the door.

Arlette entered the room like someone who had just returned from shopping. There was a pleasant commotion, a stir, like the setting down of bags and packages. But it was just her, with Dewey a step behind. Arlette said "hello" with the breath of a sentence, then went over to pick up Mitchell.

Scotty gathered the pieces of his bicycle and invited Dewey downstairs. Scotty had another bike on a new training stand. Dewey should try it. It was a contraption, a toy. It had helped him stay in shape all winter, the next best thing to actually riding on the street. He had seen it in a magazine. It was the latest, the best. Maybe Dewey wanted to order one. A pre-season sale. The two men headed down the stairway.

Arlette grinned. "Oh, he's grown so much." She held the baby up as if she were inspecting him. "One of these days," I tell Dewey. Oh, but we are too busy now, the practice and all. Then there's this mentoring program. I am just back from talking to the Girl Scouts."

"The Girl Scouts?" Katie walked to the refrigerator and opened the door. Cheese. Milk. Celery. Soda. "Can I get you something?" Only water.

"The Girl Scouts are my thing. There are just too many girls out there who think that love is the end all," said Arlette with obvious concern. "The way I see it, if I can stop just one girl from going off the deep end, then my time will have been worthwhile."

Katie imagined a Girl Scout standing by the side of a swimming pool, about to fall in.

Arlette set her water glass down. The liquid lurched up the container. "Professional women have an obligation to show some of these girls a different life. There are very talented girls out there who have no acceptable role models." She paused. "Surely, Katie you can agree with that?"

Kate went to the refrigerator to get more ice cubes. She was aware of their coldness or their hotness, of her sudden inability to distinguish between the two sensations. The cubes stuck to her fingers. She shook them off. She agreed. The world was a mess. No important role models. No surgical training for the locals in Bosnia. Save the whales too.

"Arlette, I think it's fine what you're doing. Girl Scouting is great."

Doctors

Kate looked over at Mitchell who stood beside a child's wading pool. Toy fish were all around him, red, green, blue, yellow. Summer amusement. Mitchell gave each figure a turn at being dipped into the water.

Katie tilted a bucket, slightly, a little more. Water spilled from the container and surrounded a marigold setting. The plant bent, then seemed to recover. Katie dug another hole, pulled out the loose soil. The dirt felt cool on her hands. She heard Scotty's voice, turned her head toward the house. Dewey and Scotty had just returned from a bike ride. Scotty was taking off his helmet.

They wore army tee shirts, discards bought at a surplus store. They wore the brown shirts everywhere now, to the library benefit auction, to the club. They golfed in them, dined out in them. Dewey got the idea to be fitted for small wire-rimmed glasses. A few weeks later, Scotty did the same. Their hair was cut short with clean edges. Their likeness was a sign of fraternity. It was the bravado of the Red Cross Surgical Training Team.

"Katie!" Scotty called across the yard. She collected the unplanted settings and started for the house.

"The hospital called, but just something about scheduling," she said as she came to him.

"Jack Cassel didn't call?"

"Jack Cassel?" Kate paused. "Why would Jack Cassel call?"

"You can thank Dewey for this one. He knew that you were worried. I told him that you were only consoled by experts. So Dewey asks who are the experts. That Soviet scholar came to my mind, the one you worked with for so long." Scotty smiled and began adjusting his brake cable.

He looked up. "Dewey thought we'd bring him in to teach a crash course on Bosnian politics."

Scotty was talking, but Kate no longer heard him. He gestured with the length of his arm. His head dropped slightly as he spoke. Kate remembered the hours of waiting for another phone call from Jack Cassel at her hotel room. Dr. Cassel is in a meeting. Can he return your call? When? Dr. Cassel has left for the day. Where? She remembered waiting at the university, encountering a bag lady at the bus stop.

The woman entered Katie's thoughts. She had tried not to look at her, wasn't going to speak to her. Then all at once, Katie had turned to her with a rambling detailed confession. There were gasps and sobs. The woman's eyes were soft and unchanging. Their indifference looked like earthly forgiveness. You can't stay in this neighborhood, not after dark, the woman had said. She told Katie to go home, and Katie did; she flew back to Scotty the next day.

"You called Jack Cassel at the university, Dewey?" Katie didn't believe it. Cassel wasn't an expert on the Balkans. Yugoslavia had been an independent nation under Tito, never a part of the Soviet bloc.

Dewey's smile was slanted and sheepish. "Yeah, I called him. I told his assistant that we are a team of surgeons who were contacted by the Red Cross. I said that we are flying into Sarajevo, Bosnia, to teach the local doctors how to perform emergency amputations, that their doctors aren't trained to perform the kinds of procedures that the war requires. I said that we are interested in hiring Cassel to explain the political situation." Dewey paused, as if he were wondering what else to say.

Katie looked at her husband, then at Dewey. "He's not the one you want. He doesn't know about the Balkans."

Dewey turned this way, then that. "Well, maybe so. But he can find us an expert, I'll bet. The guy's on his honeymoon so I couldn't talk to him. He's supposed to call us." Dewey took off his glasses, wiped the lenses with his shirt. He squinted in her direction.

Thank Dewey. Thank you, Dewey.

Scotty stood beside the edge of their bed with a magazine in his hands, thumbing through the pages. Did she want to buy a new sports car? He liked the e series. He leaned over to show her an advertisement. Katie glanced at the picture. A woman wearing a Santa Claus hat was seated on the driver's side. The door was open, and she was turned with her legs in front of her.

"Scotty, this whole thing seems like a dream to me." She wasn't interested in the old holiday ad.

"You don't like this car?" He stared intently at the magazine.

"Scotty, would you stop it? Would you just stop it?" She sat up in bed. "You and Dewey call a professor about what it's like to go into a civil war. Scotty, I can buy you a book. Does it occur to you at all that this is just dangerous, frighteningly dangerous?"

"People are dying," he said without looking up at her. "Cassel called Dewey's. Arlette talked to him. He said that he'd be glad to put something together for us on Bosnia. I guess that there is not much call for Soviet experts these days. We can bring him.

Katie sighed.

"By the way, Arlette wasn't too impressed with Cassel. She's amazed that somebody like him would go to China for his honeymoon. Arlette's been working to boycott their tourism because of human rights violations against baby girls." Scotty paused. "They drown them, you know."

Jack the drowner. Of course. Katie should have known by those black eyes of his. "I get a little tired of Arlette's great big world." Katie turned to her side. She would hear no more. Scotty's voice faded and was absorbed into the darkness of a dream.

Kate could see her hands on the steering wheel. The instrument panel was lit in reds and greens, and she was driving down a two-lane highway. It was evening, winter, and huge snowflakes angled into the headlights.

The air was stuffy. She rolled down a window. The snowflakes became grains of rice, as if poured from a canister, rushing into the automobile. Rice was all around her, falling around her legs, up to her chest, near her neck. She couldn't breathe. Katie sat up straight, frantically drawing her breath and could see the bedroom in shadows. Scotty was sleeping next to her. No snowflakes. No rice. Kate rested her head and now wished only for solid and uneventful sleep.

A woman walked up to Katie and shook her hand. She probably didn't remember, but they had met at the club. Katie smiled, not recognizing her. Doctors, wives, business people, seemed like shapes turning through the room, loose, then collecting into patterns as if they were images in a kaleidoscope.

Arlette stood in front of a group of men. She was talking; her mouth strained wildly at times and appeared to close with equal energy. Dewey was placing more folding chairs in the back of the hall, occasionally lifting his head to greet a colleague. Scotty was at the podium, with Jack standing beside him. Jack fumbled with papers, notes. Local broadcast journalists straightened cords and hauled lighting and sound equipment.

Katie found a seat in the back. A reporter stooped beside her. Could she identify the speaker, which man was Jack Cassel? She pointed to him and watched him talk to her husband. He wore a gray suit, the color of a mark from a sketching pencil. His hair was black, longer than in the past, and part of it fell onto his forehead.

Scotty was lighter, almost breezy in comparison. His skin and hair were a matching hue. He was casual, talkative, obviously at home in a public setting.

Scotty approached the podium, went up to introduce Jack to the audience. Then Jack's voice filled the room. Fragments from the past tumbled through her mind. Taxi drivers were the worst. Look at the mud on her skirt. Did she like chapter two, the rise of the Bolsheviks? Lenin's piercing eyes. The eyes of a revolutionary.

Did he have a sponge? She chattered. He laughed. Taxi drivers were the worst. A simple brown skirt dropped to the floor. She felt his hands on her face, on her breasts. The introduction is long. Cut it. I like Lenin's eyes. His hands were between her thighs. Maybe the last three sentences. Cut it. His mouth was on her neck. If I had a sponge. It won't stain. The last sentences. Look at the mud on her skirt. Taxi drivers were the worst. A simple brown skirt dropped to the floor.

Katie looked at Scotty, then stood and walked into the lobby. Jack's voice could still be heard but was now distant. After a while, the double doors opened. Scotty and Jack moved to the center of the entryway, trying to find her. She held up her hand to get their attention.

Excellent presentation. Did she need some air? Scotty was pleased by the turnout. Cassel was a good speaker. Scotty was glad that they went through with the idea. He put his hand on Jack's shoulder as a gesture of approval, then pointed to the drinking fountain. There was a line. Scotty smiled and walked over to it, falling into it.

Jack's eyes watched the crowd. He stood beside her. He began to rock on his heels. "I didn't know that you were married to the hero-type."

He looked down to her. "Kaytee likes the manly type." His smile was huge, brilliant, and mocking.

"Congratulations on your marriage. I've heard that you are just back from a honeymoon."

"Thank you. Are you recommending marriage these days?" Jack looked straight ahead.

Katie ignored him. He watched her now. "Rebel Kate, Katya. Uncommitted. Unaffected. Free. No strings attached. My little lover of liberty."

"I was no more free, never more free than a yo-yo. So don't abuse me."

She shook her head in disbelief and walked over to Scotty. "I want to go home."

Scotty noted the thinning crowd. "Well, just a minute. I want to thank the professor." Katie drew a breath. "Okay?"

Okay. It was finally over. She turned around; the double doors were open. Dewey and the club woman were folding chairs on opposite sides of the aisles. The hall's arrangement was disappearing before her eyes.

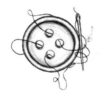

Knicks and Knacks

K atie waited by the side of the curb and anticipated chatting with the mailman about almost any mundane subject. She was suddenly aware of Mitchell's weight against her arms and adjusted him so that he rested on her hip. The jeep pulled up in front of one box, then another. She watched the vehicle roll towards her.

Inside the cab was a person she had never seen before. Katie was let down by the unexpected face. Still, he greeted her, smiled, and gave her several letters. She separated an envelope from the stack. "A letter from Daddy," she told Mitchell, who had an arm out for the rubber band.

Now inside the kitchen, Katie set the mail down on the counter and went to the cupboard for animal crackers. She looked at her son. He was interested. Bears. Tigers. Camels. Elephants. Katie poured the baked creatures onto the table and returned to Scotty's letter, opening it, drawing out the pages:

Kosevo Hospital
Sarajevo, Bosnia

Dear Katie,

I hope you and Mitchell are doing fine. As for me, I can't wait to be home again. Thank goodness that we should be through here in a few weeks.

I have been working without much sleep. Guns fire on Sarajevo from the surrounding mountains and the noise is endless. Every day brings more victims.

Last night, actually this morning, I operated on a man by the name of Mujo Hadzanagic. There was no time for X-rays, and I made a decision to amputate his left leg without them. It seems that I am training myself to do things as I have never done them.

The power went out. I nurse held a flashlight over my shoulder. She was sobbing all the while. I was finished at 2AM. At 5AM, he died. This isn't surgery. It is more like operating a surgical saw with crossed fingers. Nothing goes the way I expect. No one even has called about this man. What good is expertise in these circumstances?

Faruk Kulenovic, the head Kosevo surgeon, is grateful for the assistance. He performed the 60th amputation of his career recently. Is it not odd that he keeps track?

Marko Vukovic and Dewey went into the Buka Potok district. This area has been hit hard by artillery and tanks since Wednesday. I haven't heard from them yet and feel that someone should have by now. Still don't mention this to Arlette. I am sure they are just delayed.

Only four more weeks of this! I bought you a dress when we were stopped in Paris and can't wait for you to see the colors.

Love, Scotty

The letter rested on Katie's knee. It was so unlike Scotty to mention his concern, his worry about anything. That fact made her believe that Dewey's lack of communication was really more than a delay. Kate noted the handwriting on the envelope and was reminded about how long it had been since Scotty had sent her a letter. His last year of school, he had often sent her notes to open at her desk. She observed the slant of the S. She stood and walked to the telephone.

"Orthopedic Associates." A woman's voice was on the line.

"May I speak to Dr. White?" The voice snipped back that she needed to say which Dr. White; there were two, and one of them was out of town.

"This is Katie Tinsman. If Arlette isn't too busy, would you put her on?"

Arlette picked up the receiver. Katie began speaking. "I just opened a letter from Scotty. I want to know who your contact person is with the Red Cross. He doesn't sound good, and I want to bring him home early."

There was a long silence. That was impossible. Arlette tried to assure her that Scotty was a surgeon and was trained for emergencies. They needed to talk more. Arlette wanted to know if she could stop by after the office closed. She was with somebody and couldn't talk.

"Arlette, I only need the name."

Arlette paused again. She said that they were scheduled to come home in a month. She thought Dewey and Scotty ought to decide if they came back early or not.

Another voice came on the line. "Mrs. Tinsman? Dr. White will have to get back with you." Katie said nothing but held the receiver away from her ear. At last, she slammed it down. Her son clung to her leg.

⌒

At six o'clock that evening Katie heard a gentle knock at the side door. Arlette let herself in, hesitating, then walking a little further until the two women met.

"Katie," Arlette said. "There you are. Sorry that I couldn't talk earlier. You can't imagine how busy I am with the guys gone."

Katie looked at her, wondering what to expect. She turned her head back into the living room: Mitchell was watching television. "What is it, Arlette?

"Katie," Arlette consoled her. "Believe me, Katie, I understand how this must seem to somebody who has never performed surgery. By what you told me, a flashlight, a nurse crying … actually it was wrong of Scotty to share those details." Arlette stopped for a minute.

"Okay. I'll just tell you how I feel about this." She watched Katie's face. "Scotty and Dewey have made a commitment to the community; they have an agreement … and they'll be expected to make good on it. It would be almost irresponsible to ask them to come back sooner than what they've agreed upon."

Katie looked at her. Arlette walked around the furniture as if it were driftwood in a fast current, meeting an obstacle, stopping, spinning, then onto somewhere else. Arlette made a way to her purse. It hung from the back of a kitchen chair. After a time, she retrieved a prescription bottle. Katie watched her pour the capsules into her hand, as if she were unsure of the number left in the container. Then Arlette sat down, holding a pill and waiting for water. "I have had a bad sinus infection," she said.

Katie took a glass from the cabinet. "The community. The community," she repeated the word just to hear it. "I don't care about that. I don't know if the community cares one way or another about what happens to Scotty and

Dewey." She laughed as if to herself. "I don't know whether or not it would matter very much if they did."

"That's thinking very young." Arlette cupped her hand more fully, put the medicine in her mouth, and reached for the water. "Do what you like. Call the Red Cross if you want. It's not for me to tell you what to do."

Arlette moved slowly to the door, like someone who wanted to make a gracious exit. She put her hand on the knob and turned her head back slightly. "By the time the arrangements can be made to bring them home early, they'll be home."

⌣

Ace, king, queen, jack. Ace, king, queen, jack. Ace, king, queen, jack. Scotty sorted through a deck of playing cards.

"Just one more game?"

Katie grinned, shook her head. She walked to the window, pulled the drapery cord to let in the light. It was morning. The neighbors had made their daily exodus into the city. She surveyed the houses, the crimson leaves that hung from the maples in the front yards. Her view followed the tree limbs to the roofs: the sky was firm and pale as if it were the shell of a bird's egg. Her gaze then fell, meeting evergreens, scarlet chrysanthemums.

She turned to Scotty who sat at a small table. She looked at his bare chest. "You're terribly underdressed," she said to her husband. She went to his closet and took out a shirt. She watched his face. "No, not blue." She returned the shirt to a hanger.

Scotty smiled. Ace, king, queen, jack. Scotty put the cards back into a deck. He sat for a minute as if he were thinking. "I don't want to go to another reception," he said as placed his arms on the wheelchair so that his elbows stuck out.

"What about Arlette?" Katie asked. Scotty pointed to the newspaper on their dresser.

Kate picked up the paper and went to the bed and sat beside him. A picture of Arlette was on the front page. The photo was taken at a receiving center for Bosnian orphans. She sat among several orphans; a curly-haired child was on her lap. The headline read: Lost Surgeon's Wife Sets Up Memorial.

Scotty shuffled the deck. "For the last month, it's been nothing but reporters. I am tired of reporters." He was silent. He held up the cards, let them fall. They fluttered all around him.

He turned to her. "You know, Katie, I went away thinking that I was going to teach them all the tricks. People were dying: I had the skills to stop it.

"I was wrong."

Why had the penalty been so great? She wanted to say that it wasn't so bad to be wrong once in a while. On boards. With cards. Real things won't be played with. Katie stood, went to the door to see if Mitchell was still sleeping. She returned and picked up the scattered deck.

"What do you want to play, Scotty?" She sat across from him at the table and began to deal.

Untitled

Audrey held Jeff's legs like they were the ladder of a swimming pool. Fine hair waved from his ankle like algae sweeping against her face. Motor boats pounded on the surf. Their distance could be heard by dull thumps.

Jeff was sitting on the dock, bent over slightly. His hands rested on the edge of its planks. She could see only his face. His shoulders fell into a shadow in front of sunlight. Jeff hoisted her with his legs, lifting, letting go. He looked up to the sky. The moon was visible. "You should write a poem about Venus." He imagined it to be evening, the way the two lights looked together.

Audrey's right hand was now free. She pinched water from her nose, then pushed her hair back. Water splashed into her mouth. She pulled herself higher to his calf. "Oh, Hesperus and Phosphorus …" Audrey kissed his leg. She laughed. "Tell me, Mr. Galileo, what do you see in that star? Do you want to talk about love, dear sir?" She could see him smile. She put her finger on her lip. "Is there not a star that burns hotter than the evening star?"

Jeff blushed. He lifted one leg onto the dock, then wrapped his arms around it. The wind parted his blond hair into sections. Audrey reached up to a warped plank.

"I have always thought it was pretty. It's predictable. It's often beside the moon. The surface is cloud-covered; so it's a mystery too."

Audrey could tell that he thought he had revealed too much. He looked like a boy who had been kissed by an elderly aunt. Jeff stood, leaned over, put out his hand to her. "You are going to be a prune."

Her legs were taut against a rusty barrel. He pulled her from the water. It rushed from her bathing suit, then trickled down her skin. He handed her a towel. "It's probably time to eat."

Jeff's father had taken over a table in the center of the room. He read a newspaper. A stack of unread editions were beside his arm, the *Courier,* the *Sentinel,* the *Journal.* A pair of drugstore glasses rested on his nose. A three-candidate gubernatorial race had his attention. He read the county polls like a horse enthusiast before the Kentucky Derby, trying to put the statistics together into a comfortable place to put his money. The attorney general had attacked the corporate climate, but was popular. The lt. governor had only two years of experience. The speaker of the house already had a hefty treasury. Harrison had been around the political world enough to know that you had to pick the winner before the election.

His mother moved back and forth from the refrigerator to the stove. The cabin smelled like battered pike. It sizzled in the deep fryer. Rose turned quickly. "You are just in time to make the salad." She tossed a head of lettuce at her son, an unopened bag of carrots at her daughter-in-law.

"Jeff, look at your shoulders." She opened a drawer, removed a tube of ointment, and unscrewed the top. "You shouldn't stay in the sun so long. Any doctor will tell you that." She rubbed his skin gently, around the shoulder blades, up to the base of his neck. She replaced the cap, then walked to the sink to wash her hands. Rose's voice softened. "Did you kids have fun?"

Audrey looked at the carrots, then at Jeff. He took them from her so that she could change her clothes. Jeff walked to the counter. "The water is really warm." He set the vegetables down.

"It's only June." His mother handed him a knife. "Don't cut the carrots in chunks. They are too hard to chew." She looked over at her husband. "I remember once, when you were little, you nearly choked on a piece of cut apple." She smiled at the wisdom she had acquired over the years, then set a bag of radishes in front of her son. There was a long silence. Rose watched her son. Her hands were tucked in the pockets of a red golf skirt. "Jeff?" He looked at her briefly. "A gal in my bridge club read Audrey's story. Oh, what's the name of that magazine?" He didn't answer. Carrots rolled like coins, a short distance on the cutting board. She took a dish towel from the handle of the refrigerator.

Audrey came down the steps. Her hair was black like the surface of coal from dampness. It fell at one length slightly above the middle of her neck. "Oh, there you are," Rose said. "I was just telling Jeff about your story. Madeline, from my card club read it. She was a little confused. It seemed so gloomy to her." Rose twisted the orange-colored print. "You know, sad."

Jeff's mother put the towel back and handed Audrey two tomatoes. She walked to a tote bag set beside the table. "Audrey dear, this is my favorite author. She writes mysteries, nice stories, like Agatha Christie's." She held the book out, as if it were being displayed.

"Rose, I can't concentrate." Harrison lifted his eyes above the bifocals. He took a rubber band from a folded paper.

Rose looked over to him. Her mouth opened as if she were going to say something. Jeff interrupted. "Audrey's work is different, mother." His knife cracked against the cutting board. "So what if the bridge club thought it was gloomy? Maybe they don't read much literature?" Audrey looked for the tongs for the salad, staring into a drawer.

"There is no need to get hoity-toity about it. Audrey is like a daughter to me." She walked to Audrey. She lowered her voice to a whisper, the way one comments about another in the person's presence. "Why in the world would a girl like you write about incest?" Audrey tore some lettuce. Jeff set the knife down, resigned, in disbelief.

Audrey smiled. "I think because it happens," she said gently. The bowl was almost full. "When you write, you …"

Rose didn't want to hear it. "Many things happen in this world, but we don't go passing them off as entertainment. Bad news is everywhere. Orphans, for instance, it is so sad." There was no reaction. She looked at the couple's faces. They seemed to ignore her. Rose wadded a wrapper. "But leave it to the sociologists, for crying out loud. Harrison and I have worked hard to get where we are."

"Rose, shut up," Harrison said over his paper. It fell beneath his chin. "Leave the poor girl alone," he said softy.

"No, I won't leave her alone." She slammed the cabinet door. "She says she writes about the world. Does anyone ever play golf, have a couple of drinks with friends, or do anything besides moan about the human condition, as she puts it? She doesn't write about my world. Everybody feels too much, cries too much, and even for God's sake loves too much in some perverse sort of way. Then everyone says what's wrong with your daughter-in-law? Is Jeff's marriage okay? Where does she ever come up with those ideas?" She threw up her arms, then sank into a chair.

Jeff put his hands on both sides of Audrey's waist, as if she could be rolled out of the room with a little push. "Let's go outside." He eased her in the direction of the door.

As Audrey stepped out onto the porch, she heard their voices rise in sharp peaks, then fall into silence. She imagined Harrison removing another rubber band, reporting Johnson county was another disappointment. They had the most to lose by electing an environmentalist. Rose would soon go upstairs to sulk. It seemed that everything and nothing had happened at once, like the significance of a world champion boxing match.

Jeff walked out from the kitchen. His white swimming trunks made his legs look skinny. He shut the door, making sure the latch was clasped. He sat beside Audrey on a bench. A cool wind blew across the lake. Jeff shook. "I'm sorry," he said.

Audrey touched the back of his head. Her fingers brushed up the short hair. "I was going to tell your mother that when you write, people seem to drop steamer trunks at your feet, but they open them. Some throw out silk first. Others throw out patched cotton. No matter what the order, the content is still the same." She paused. "I was at a book fair in Athens, Ohio, when an older girl told me that her father had raped her while her mother nursed her baby sister." Jeff was blank. "It spins around and around in your thoughts for hours. You could hear sales representatives saying 'have a nice day' to customers." She looked at her husband. "And I wished that I had known something that polite and invisible to say to that child."

Light rippled on the lake. Green and red navigation signals blinked in the distance. Jeff leaned his head back into her lap. "Jeff?"

"Uh, huh?"

"Tell me about Mercury."

What Little
Eyes Can See

Matt dipped a spoon into the sugar bowl. The three sat around the kitchen table waiting for the cake to cool. It was a white cake shaped like a lamb. The mother pushed the cream closer to her son. Her hair was graying without the loss of youth's lustre. The strands were strong and glistened in the fluorescent light. Katherine filed her nails. Then after the quick bits of motion, she stretched her fingers out like a web to note the improvement. She set the file down. "I need to call the airport," she said. Matt stirred his coffee. "Where's your telephone book?"

He stood, turned to the cabinet behind him, then tossed the book onto the table. Katherine flipped through the pages. "A friend might have a job for me with a cosmetics company." She did not look up at them. "Oh look, you have Lucky Ducks here too. I thought it was a regional franchise."

Matt watched his sister. She wore a peach-colored dress. A gold bracelet sloshed on her wrist. Her eyes were blue. Traces of smiles were drawn around their edges. Her hair fanned back from her face. Matt thought she looked out of place, much the way a leopard would look on a city street.

"Katherine," the mother scolded. "The lamb is barely out of the oven. I haven't put the coconut on yet and you talk about home." She pointed to the pan that held the cake. Matt poured himself more coffee. "When you were a little girl, you always put the eyes on the lamb. Oh, mama, you would say, I want that little lamb to see. The mother moved to one corner of the room. "You would stand on a green stool next to the counter like you were big enough to see the world." Katherine smiled. "Then you would pick the color of jelly beans for the lamb's eyes. The mother looked at her daughter. Katherine seemed to remember, but the woman was unsure. The older woman's eyebrows knitted slightly, then fell back into soft crescents.

Matt brushed his hair to the side. "I thought you had some business to take care of?" His face was stern. It warned her not to leave town without making a decision about their mother. "You had to see your attorney, didn't you? Something about your divorce settlement?" The mother walked to the stove, then placed her hands on each side as if she would move it. Her eyes were fixed on the cake. The divorce had bothered her. She would not interfere.

Katherine groaned. She looked at Matt. "A job is a job," she said cheerfully. She lifted her chin and shook her head. "I must leave right after Easter." The mother leaned against the stove. Her arms were now folded. "I will have been here for two weeks then. A lot can happen in Los Angeles in that time. In my line of work, you just can't do as you please."

Matt heard his mother mumble. She poured jelly beans onto a plate. Two or three bounced on the linoleum, then rolled across the floor. A red bean came to rest behind a chair. "Today is Maundy Thursday," the mother said. Matt's eyes shot to his sister. He tapped a teaspoon on the table anticipating the next words that his mother would say. "Do you remember what happened on Maundy Thursday?" Katherine's head moved nervously about the room looking for a place to put her attention. Matt wanted to tell her that it was the day that we remembered Jesus' washing of the disciples' feet. He leaned back into his chair, one arm on the table, the other behind him. Let Katherine hear for herself.

His mother started. Her voice was steady, sad. "Paul was driving the cattle truck home from St. Louis. He was just past Pilot Knob. It was late. He was probably tired." The old woman began to sob. "A freight train hit his truck at a crossing." She grasped the edge of the counter. "He died on Good Friday. He would have been buried on Easter Sunday." Matt shut his eyes. He held his hand over the coffee cup. He could feel the steam, the heat …

᠆

Matt leaned against the mailbox, a post stuck in the ground beside a tar road. The heat was visible and rose like gasoline fumes from the spout of an open can. The tar blistered and pocked from the July sun. A girl about ten stood beside him. Matt kicked the dead animal. Its body felt no different than a ball much to the boy's surprise. Katherine swung her head back and forth as if the rebuke were mechanical. "If you do that again, I'm going to tell."

The younger brother looked up the hill where his grandparents lived. Tree trunks jutted from the ground like huge lead rods against a green canvass. The smell of ragweed hung in the brush.. An animal scurried.

He stuck his foot out again, close to the opossum. "It's dead. It's not going to hurt you." Matt slid his boot in loose gravel. "What's wrong? Are you scared of an ole dead possum?"

The girl stepped into the road. "How do you know it's dead? It might just be pretending so you'll go away and leave it alone." She smiled. Her point was made.

Matt studied the body. It was dead. "Ah, go on. Sure it's dead." He brought his heel down close to the tail. What if it wasn't? He imagined it snapping at his ankle. He pushed his foot down closer. He would touch it. He heard his Uncle

Paul's voice call from the top of the hill. Katherine's hair was aflame with sunlight. It was time to come in.

↩

Moisture had condensed on his palm. He heard Katherine. "Mama, that was a long time ago. You mustn't let it upset you so. Matt's eyes were still closed. "Mama?" Katherine's tone lifted. "Let's put on the lamb's wool? It will be fun. Here's the coconut." She put the bag next to the cake. Her expression became childish, big and rounded. "I think the lamb should have lavender eyes." She sorted through the candy beans. "These two are perfect. Look, Mama, they are perfect." Katherine looked over at Matt. "Don't you think so, Matty?"

Matt turned. "Why not? You see them every day, don't you?" Katherine ignored him. Matt watched the surface of the liquid in his cup as if it would swallow him, take him away. He had heard his mother's Easter story for twenty-five years. In this time, only once did he feel sorrow. He was nine. It scared him when he was a child, as most children fear hints of injustice. It had bored him. It had made him feel guilty, a worn sympathy that couldn't hurt anymore than does a callous on a construction worker's hand. He couldn't feel it anymore. It was this that made him want to scream inside, to be human, to feel inhumane.

He could hear his mother describe the accident scene. Each year this part of the story became more vivid. The cab had been thrown farther. The metal was more completely crushed. Her brother's body more mangled. His arm had been found underneath the seat. Her red-headed brother's hair appeared black from coagulated blood. She would recount the train's schedules, when the whistles could be heard in Caldonia. It seemed that she could hear the locomotion, the rocking boxcars, and the impact. Matt was sure that his mother had slowly gone mad. Katherine's voice, its sweet, patronizing tone irritated. He turned the spoon in his cup. Katherine wanted to do nothing. It was his problem. He was responsible. Mother was old.

The story ended with a bit about his grandmother. She no longer recited "Evangeline" after Paul's death. Mother couldn't remember who wrote the poem, or even what the poem was about. Sometimes she said Hawthorne, others, Longfellow. Matt swung his head back to Katherine. Now she looked like a plow horse on a historical postcard. She was still out of place. The title of the poem went through his head. It was a woman's name. Perhaps Evangeline had been a woman who had never suffered loss, a gay woman who still dreamed, who was vibrant and alive. He imagined the poem to be beautiful, something that his grandmother loved as much as her son.

Matt turned back to his mother. She was tired. Her hair was like braids of silk pinned at the back of her head. Her eyes were dark, appearing almost hollow, drained with grief. She would rest now. Katherine led her down the hallway to a bedroom. She would spend the night. Katherine told her mother that everything was okay. Matt saw that the telephone book was still open to airlines. She walked into the kitchen. "You are a real prick," Katherine said softly. She tore the seal on the coconut bag. She dabbed coconut onto the frosting.

"She's lost her grip, Kass." He tried to meet her eyes. She evaded him. "She has told the story five times since Lent.

Her grief is becoming more intense." He wanted Katherine to look at him. She wouldn't. "She relives it, Kass." His eyes begged her to look at him.

"She is your mother." The lamb's fleece was splotchy. She evened it out. "You want to put her in an institution." Katherine squashed the lamb's nose. "I won't see your lawyer. She is an old woman."

"A nursing home is not an insane asylum," he growled. His wire glasses slid down his nose. There was a long silence. Matt knew that the conversation had ended. Katherine would go back to Los Angeles. Her letters would continue to report trips to the grape vineyards, mud baths, and baseball games. She had dated a minor league right-fielder last year.

"Matty, hold the plate for me. I want to put in the eyes." She turned the platter. "Would you put them in? I have frosting on my hands." Matt took the shiny beans in his hands. He placed one, then the other on the lamb's face. Katherine smiled. The clock struck midnight. It was done.

Matt lay on the couch. The radio played Van Morrison. Why had he not persisted? He heard the wind whistle through the eaves … It whipped his hair. "Why can't we go inside? I'm cold." Katherine shivered and stood beside the house. He tucked his hands into a miniature Navy dress coat. His white shirt was last year's and tugged at his wrists when he moved. Matt could hear voices in the house that rose between long pauses. If it had been summer, he would have been down at the creek.

"We could go sit in the car." Kass pointed to the black sedan parked at the crest of the hill. "Daddy said that they're grieving Uncle Paul. He'll call us." Matt turned to see the fields that appeared like an arena enclosed by old mountains. Clouds rested on their rounded, weathered peaks. "They aren't going to leave us out here all day."

Matt walked to the spring house and came back with a bucket. He brought it to the porch, turned it upside down, stood on it to see in the window. The wind stung the backs of his legs through his trousers. He could see his mother. Her plaid dress looked like a patchwork quilt thrown on the floor. Her brown braids were like the rope of a tire swing, taut hemp burning against flesh that one could not let go of nor hang on to. His grandmother tried to move her to a chair. Finally his father lifted her.

⌒

He saw the reflection of the strange creature with lavender eyes in the window. The news break had ended. It was Good Friday. He heard the minister's chant: "Lamb of God who takes away the sins of the world. Have mercy on us. Lamb of God who takes away the sins of the world. Have mercy ..." Matt turned the radio off.

Matt walked into the kitchen, opened another bag of jelly beans. He found two black ones. Matt put them in place of the others, then stood back. The shiny licorice eyes might now see.

Another Manhattan Project

Susan's fingers hit the keys of the Smith-Corona. It was like a relic from a lost civilization, maybe high school. Danny was behind her with Jacob. She could her the hotel's cleaning crew in the hall, vague voices. Jacob babbled. Danny swayed back and forth in an attempt to quiet the two-year old.

```
THE 1963 PARTIAL TEST BAN TREATY
THAT WAS NEGOTIATED BY PRESIDENT
KENNEDY DID NOT TAKE INTO ACCOUNT
TESTING WEAPONS UNDERGROUND. THE NON-
PROLIFERATION TREATY IS UP FOR SENATE
REVIEW IN 1990. WITH THIS REVIEW, I
BELIEVE THAT IT IS TIME TO STOP GLOBAL
RADIATION CONTAMINATION. EIGHTEEN
HUNDRED UNDERGROUND TEST EXPLOSIONS ...
```

"How long do you think this is going to take?" Danny was restless. She stopped typing, then looked back to him. Jacob pulled a baseball hat down over his eyes. "Susan, don't make the speech too long or even the people in the first row will fall asleep." Jacob pounded on his chest. "Senators are known for their long-winded speeches. They read telephone books, don't they?" Jacob howled.

"Look Danny." Susan put her hand on her forehead. "I didn't know I was going to have to work so much. I can't predict deadlines." She turned to the typewriter, then back to Danny. "If the Senator wants to talk about strontium in mother's milk, he does. The Soviet test forces us to change the speech. It's a peace convention, Danny." Jacob screeched. She looked to her son. He supported his weight against Danny's belt like a cowboy in stirrups. "We did spend all yesterday together." She turned back to the typewriter.

```
A COMPREHENSIVE TEST BAN TREATY IS
THE ONLY VIABLE SOLUTION, ONE THAT
IS VERIFIABLE, THAT ULTIMATELY WORKS
TOWARD THE ELIMINATION OF ALL NUCLEAR
WEAPONS TESTING. WE CAN NO LONGER
ASSUME THAT ...
```

"I am not going to stay in this room all day," said Danny. He pulled Jacob's coat from the closet. "It makes me too damned nervous. Susan did not look at him. "We're going for a walk ... maybe to the art museum. Okay?"

```
WE NEED TO THINK IN TERMS OF GLOBAL
PROLIFERATION. IRAN, LIBYA ...
```

"Yes, yes. Go on. The convention's not until seven. I'm going to run this over to the Central office around four." Jacob darted across the floor. He had found a towel and wrapped it around his head. "The Senator needs some time to feel comfortable with the changes."

Danny and Jacob had left. The room was silent. Susan set the alarm clock for quarter of four. She reread the memorandum. The Senator wanted a more sincere tone. United Peace had raised eighty thousand at one fund-raiser alone. Do not mention Israel. Be wary of environmental promises. Mention radioactive contamination only as it pertains to PTB Treaty. Make reference to the Senator's sons. Acknowledge the United Nations frequently. Stress verification in all test ban treaties.

Jacob's bottle lay on the floor. Susan could now decipher the wallpaper, tropical birds in palm trees. The busy pattern disclosed itself only to the most interested eye. The typewriter hummed. She imagined Danny at the art institute with Jacob. Susan had meant the weekend to be fun.

MY SON BRIAN IS NOT HERE TODAY BECAUSE
OF PEACE CORPS DUTY IN HONDURAS.

Who would have thought it would be like this?

STEVE IS AN ORDAINED MINISTER IN NEW
HAVEN, CONNECTICUT. HIS WIFE, BETH ...

Danny expected too much.

GREG IS A LITTLE LEAGUE BASEBALL COACH
WHO PRACTICES LAW.

He acted childish.

I AM PROUD OF MY FAMILY AND BELIEVE
THAT THEY HAVE A BIRTHRIGHT TO PEACE.
THE THREAT OF NUCLEAR WAR ...

Don't inconvenience him for one lousy hour. Susan's neck grew stiff. Blood rushed her cheeks. Parrots with cinder-black eyes seemed to mock her from their perch on the wallpaper.

PEACE IS A COMMITMENT. IT IS THE
PROCESS. IT IS THE GOAL ...

She looked at the copy. The travel alarm ticked. Keys began to fire on white paper, black ink. Her face burned with anger.

... EXPLOSION WAS A VIOLATION OF
EXISTING TEST BAN TREATIES.

The alarm rang. Its vibration seemed to shake the desk. Susan finished the paragraph. The typewriter's carriage shot back, return. She looked at the clock. The Senator wanted the speech at four. Close it.

⌣

The convention center's walkway sloped down into an area divided by rectangular tables. A speaker's platform was in the center of the room. White linen tablecloths shimmered under the fluorescent lights. Small groups of people entered the hall like driftwood caught in waves, flux and pause, flux and pause. Women dressed in magenta and teal strolled the aisles checking delegates'credentials. Susan stood at the entrance. A large woman with over-ratted hair took tickets from registrants who wished to win centerpieces. Her heaping body looked as though it had been placed on a Sunday school chair. She held a book in her hands, *The Collected Short Stories of Katherine Mansfield.*

Fiction. Susan watched the platform. The hotel electricians tested the wires to the microphone. The press had begun to arrive, clinking, clanking, video equipment behind London Fog overcoats. Young reporters stood behind a section rope like children at a circus, bewildered, excited. She could see the Senator between black suits. His cropped white hair wiggled as he talked to members of the Central staff. Waitresses delivered pitchers of cocktails to selected tables, martinis, manhattans. An usher motioned her to the front. The Senator's eyes strayed from another conversation. She met them like a guilty lover, an understated intimacy. The delegates were seated. Susan poured herself a drink.

Words reeled through her head. The Senator approached the podium. The people next to her wintered in Florida, winter as a verb. Conversations fused into noise. A woman began to speak. Susan listened to the woman's introduction. The Senator's voice rolled through her thoughts. She could hear her own words. They stepped by her, one by one, into rote nonsense.

```
THE NUCLEAR ARMS RACE ...
```

Susan's finger's tapped the table. His inflection was better, stressed syllables drawn to meaning, a portrayal of dignity, ownership.

```
I BELIEVE THAT IT IS TIME TO STOP
GLOBAL RADIATION/CONTAMINATION.
```

She poured herself another drink.

The ticket lady had joined the delegation. She self-consciously moved between tables, trying not to be a distraction. Susan saw the book in her hands, a picture of Katherine Mansfield on the cover. Was she going to read it? Didn't she care about the Senator's speech? The woman opened the book. Susan looked to the Senator. His voice rose and sank like a corked bottle at sea. The audience applauded. The woman continued to read. The man beside her held a child on his lap like a doll in a calico jumpsuit. He whispered to the child. The child whispered back.

```
MY SON BRIAN IS NOT HERE TODAY BECAUSE
OF PEACE CORPS DUTY IN HONDURAS.
```

The microphone squealed like laughter.

Susan poured herself another drink.

⌒

Susan turned the doorknob and quietly removed the key. Jacob stirred. She ducked into the bathroom. Danny's and Jacob's bathing suits hung from the towel rack. An occasional drop of water fell to the floor. Jacob's bottle was in the bathtub. How long had they been sleeping? One heel went off, then the other, then the rest of her clothing. Susan slipped a nightgown on. She could hear Danny breathing, heavy from sleep. She walked into the darkness, followed the corners of Jacob's bed to Danny.

The sheets were warm, her eyes open. Clipped images entered her mind. She imagined parrots on their perch, ridiculous birds with cinder-black eyes. The ticket lady. Magenta and teal. Mansfield's eyes, dark, penetrating. Magenta and teal. Men in black suits …

"Danny?" He didn't answer. "Danny?" She came closer to him, her breasts against his back. "Do you know what I really want?" She paused. "I want to write a great book … move to London … maybe lecture at Oxford … once." She listened. "I want to sleep with you in the afternoon." Jacob stirred. "I want to be out of town when the best people call."

"Susan, it's late. Can we talk about it tomorrow?" He moved to the edge of the mattress, then pulled a pillow into his arms. His breathing, its swell, carried her as if into a vortex, into the deep, undefined darkness of sleep.

Deciphering
Norelco

I squinted my eyes. They were the color of a shady pond then. They are darker now. My nose was fine and delicate like a handle on a teacup. My hair was wavy, coarse, matching the deep rust of a rotting log.

I pulled back on my fishing line as if the motion would prompt a quick decision by underwater onlookers. No bites. No luck. What if I pulled back twice, fast, jerky motions? Fishing was a superstitious pastime.

I scrutinized the steps taken by an old man on the pier across from me. The pier, as the patrons called it, was a rickety structure, a long arrangement of planks, fastened to posts, and held by the mire. Its planks were bowed and curled around their edges, softly gray.

Dubie Ostermann was an ancient fellow and walked in stiff, unmeasured steps. His eyes looked like erasers on the end of pencils. Above these circular spaces were white eyebrows, and they clung to his forehead as if they were caterpillars on the light side of a leaf. He hobbled. He hunched. He hadn't been anywhere besides the river. I felt certain about that.

The tale was that Ostermann was born on the island between the slough and the tavern. It was a dark enough, eerie enough place that such a character might have entered the world there. The patrons said that Ostermann was raised by a primitive family, the last of the primitives.

All this made sense to me. I was twelve years old. And in those twelve years, I had never seen him drive a car. He didn't own a refrigerator or any type of electric appliance. He kept his milk in the coolers at the tavern. He didn't have a telephone. A bait bucket, filled with leeches, sat on the porch at the back of his cabin. To my horror, Ostermann even ate what he pulled from the river, gar, carp, and an occasional catfish.

Dubie Ostermann almost had the tackle out of the boat. He cussed. He glared. I predicted that soon he would disappear into his shack. The house itself was faintly yellow, not as a chosen color, but as a result of worn paint. An outboard motor, without an engine cover, was clamped to a wooden stand beside the shed. There was no grass. The ground was smooth and cracked like geographic boundaries on a travel map. The flood water had receded.

Beside Ostermann's house was the tavern. Its exterior was clad in sandy roof-like siding. A pickup truck, with a rusty and smashed fender, overtook the parking lot much like an animal with a will to dominate all space. I heard laughter, strange cackling laughter, coming from the bar. A patron yelled something that I couldn't understand. I turned back to the pier.

"Why don't you go home? Do you have a home? You really shouldn't be hanging around this place. There's trouble here." Dubie Ostermann was talking to me. I heard his oddly unfamiliar voice. I again heard the laughter coming from the tavern. Why didn't he mind his own business?

"I fish here all the time," I said. "It's okay. I'm not hurting anything." My head turned to the bar. My insides shook. "I stock coolers for Mr. Van Acker on Saturday mornings." I was finally impressed by my own pleas of legitimacy. A scowl still was on the old man's face.

"Go on home. This ain't no place for you." His head swung back and forth. A skinny mongrel followed him down the pier. It bobbed and jittered with excitement. The dog anticipated the visceral delights from the morning's catch. I knew that it was the primitive's pet.

I shoved dirt down from the riverbank into the water with the heel of my tennis shoe. It crumbled like exploding debris in the scene of a movie. The sky was white and blank. I could hear semitrailers whining beyond the trees. I heard the laughter. A woman came out from the bar. I reeled in my fishing line, grabbed my jacket, and ran to the parking lot. Mr. Van Acker could be talked to later, maybe tomorrow. Now I would go home.

⌒

Farley Van Acker hugged me. "When I was your age, I swore up and down to mighty Moses that I'd own a whole block of land. Do you know the story of Moses?" Farley didn't wait for me to reply. "I just brought my sixth house down from the city. That makes me a landlord. You didn't know that Farley was going to be a millionaire, did you?" I smiled and moved away from him. I would stock the coolers.

Another patron whispered my way. "Don't let him fool you. Farley Van Acker is a windbag. They are going to hang him at an airport someday." The man shaped his lips as if he were going to blow the seeds of a spent dandelion.

I removed the already cold six-packs and set them on the floor. A small blond-haired guy began to count straws from the drinks he had had: "*Eins, zwei, drei, vier, fünf, sechs, …*" He finally stopped and began again.

The patron lowered his voice even more. I could barely hear. "That one over there thinks he's Adolf Hitler. His mind is mush. They say he's never even been to Germany, just kind of an idiot." The patron put his hand in front of my face.

"See this ring. My daddy gave it to me. My daddy was a big man. He owned an oil rig in Texas. Honor. That's what it is all about. There are four rubies and two diamonds set in this ring. Do you want me to leave it to you when I die? Would you like that?"

I nodded without looking at him. I could hear the idiot counting straws. I needed to concentrate on stacking the containers. Then Farley yelled.

"Your daddy, hell! You ain't got no daddy. You got that ring from your last wife. What was her name? Diane? Darla? Donna? Don't hold your breath waiting for that ring. That joe there ain't never going to die. That one is already pickled." The crowd roared. They hooted.

"Hey, what do you want to be when you grow up," the patron asked.

Farley yelled across the bar. "The kid wants to be exactly like you." Once again the barroom rocked with laughter. I folded the empty cartons. Mr. Van Acker gave me two silver dollars. I took a strawberry soda from a different section of the cooler. I went outside. It was late afternoon.

❧

Dubie Ostermann never came out this time of day. I imagined that he slept. He was probably stretched out on a cot on the floor. Its threads were broken. It stunk from dampness and mildew. Anyway, now was a good time to stand on the old man's pier. I had wondered what one could see from its point. It would be okay. I wouldn't stay there long, only long enough to say that once I stood on the primitive's dock in broad daylight.

Once upon the planks, the pier and its narrow walkway seemed like a road. It would lead me, if just for a moment, to someplace I hadn't seen, a place, a different place without the others. Gulls shot into the crests of waves. The river's current rushed around the posts and separated the water into two streams, then back into a single flow.

Ain't no place for you. Honor. Do you know the story of Moses? Honor. That makes me a landlord. *Eins, zwei, drei* … Ain't no place for you. Do you have a home? Would you like that? Honor. Exactly like you … like you. I heard the cabin's door, its latch, its spring. The primitive was standing behind me. I did not look back, but lifted my arms overhead and was at once in the river.

I pulled myself onto the island. I wasn't sure how long I had been in the water. The current was too strong and I had given up trying to swim against it. A dusky light was descending on the waterway and nothing seemed very real. My muscles ached. My clothes were heavy with silt. I would stay here until morning, then catch a ride back with a fisherman.

I sat for a short while. The fallen house was on this island, the one that Ostermann had been born in. Above the brush, I could see a chimney. It was built of gray stone. As I moved closer I could see the remains of a foundation made of the same material.

One wall, constructed of wood, was still in place. Charred beams were angled across the floor. Junk was scattered everywhere, a metal cup, pieces of glass, and a bent picture frame. There were tears of fabric, now black, all black. I saw an electrical cord and followed it to the body of a man's razor. The patrons were wrong. I stuffed the cord into my pocket. A boat was coming.

I saw red and green running lights on the water. It moved slowly. The engine sputtered on account of its pace. They had reported me missing. They were going to drag the slough. They had seen me go into the river. It was the sheriff's patrol. I shuddered. Or maybe it was Dubie Ostermann wanting to punish me for standing on his dock.

The engine stopped. I waited silently. I couldn't be sure. A glint of light was on the boat's metal hull. Somebody was walking across its bottom, clumsy thuds. A can was opened.

"You know, honey, I just brought my sixth house down from the city. That makes old Farley a landlord. I'm going to be a millionaire one of these days." There was a pause and then the strange laughter.

"When Farley's having a good time, his friends will have a good time too. I am a rich man. And tonight there's nobody out here but you and me."

I heard the trucks whine, their wail, the laughter. I laid back into the weeds. My fingers went into my ears. All I could see was a couple of stars being passed by tree branches. I imagined primitives perched in the boughs above. They were fierce warriors without any quality of mercy. One had to be especially quiet, or they would be alerted.

The moon's light caught the back of a leaf. It first seemed like a silver dollar hanging in the air. But that would not work. It was an arrowhead, finely sculpted, waiting to strike me. Dubie Ostermann wasn't really raised by primitives—I remembered the coins in one pocket and the razor's cord in the other. A great dark limb, a thick horizontal line, moved like a pendulum overhead. And I wondered why could it not have been so.

The Confirmation

In the darkness, he walked down an asphalt lane. Rain tapped the fallen oak leaves, as if they could be awakened to their previous glory of being a part of what was tall and majestic. The smell of wet earth stuck in the air, a smell that reminded one of construction upheaval. He passed his hand across his face. Water clung to his skin. For a moment, he was aware of his own scent. He could see the house.

The sight of the house evoked his appeal. He began his apologies. He outlined his thoughts the way a public official does before a persuasive speech. The tone could not be self-serving. He could not be abrupt or speak so rapidly as to appear thoughtless. But for all the preparation, he wondered what words he would hear in the sound of his own voice when the perfect plea left his thoughts and stumbled into something that was audible. The stamina of illusion let him continue.

If he could capture the sincerity he felt, she would listen. Who she was was insignificant. Although he had told himself this often, he did not believe the words that he offered to himself as a substitute for distasteful conclusions. Still, some alliances went beyond the guidelines of social institutions, of what is dictated and of what is dreamed. Above all else, there was hope.

Wet and determined, he pushed the doorbell. As if an alarm sounded in his heart, all seemed at stake in this courageous moment. He felt like a condemned man awaiting his destiny. The door opened. He was ushered in by a grandmother with a knitted craft in her hand. She looked at him with the indifference of one who is interrupted. She cared nothing for him, or for anyone who would make her abandon her monotony. He was left alone.

Heels moved down a marble staircase. The brush of soles on wool carpet made him aware of the urgent moment. The latch of French doors opened. In an instant, his senses were made electric by initial fear and emergent courage. He was on. But she spoke first.

"You are wet, Tom. You look cold too. I hope Grandma didn't keep you on the step long," she stated as a question.

The unmistakable care in her voice allowed him relief. "A big oak tree was struck by lightning and fell across your drive. My car is about a half-mile down the road." He looked directly at her. "Maggie, I had to talk to you."

She met his eyes with her own. She was now aware of his anxiety. His hair fell in vertical bands on his forehead. He looked beaten. She assumed power by the cast of his absurdity. The tree that had fallen could be taken care of and was of little interest to her now.

"The rain would have let up. You could have waited or even called," she said with the hope of detecting the motive for the strangely timed visit.

"I have talked to the others. It seems we will not have the numbers to confirm Jay's nomination. While it's true that I am a party leader, I am just one legislator. I have tried every argument to persuade the others, but there is a feeling that we need a commissioner from the southern part of the state."

He watched her eyes. There was no reaction, neither compassion nor disappointment. There was no perceivable design in the eyes that could be as stirring and lucid as strained tea. He could wait no longer. He had to talk. "Maggie, I know that you are disappointed. There are just too many aspects, political aspects that cannot be controlled. I have tried."

She sensed his defeat. He wanted forgiveness. For a moment she pitied him like a stray animal willing to stand patiently for anything that might be given, thrown, or held back. "Well, I guess I am disappointed. Jay deserves that appointment. Sometimes things don't work out the way that we would have them though." She turned her back to him and watched the pendulum of the wall clock swing to the rhythm of the bursts of rain.

In his mind, he asked her to come to Washington with him. He told her about the seminar. He would find time to be with her. He would make love to her, as no one ever had, including the ever-important Jay, while her husband courted every bargain of womanhood. He wanted to hold her, to touch her face, and to vent the silent and strained emotion within him.

She turned to him. "Thanks for coming out in such nasty weather. You know, Tom, you could have told me over the telephone, but I do appreciate that you came to the house. The fallen tree made the effort so much more valiant," she said as one who understood her power. "Jay will have it moved. We can't always have what we want in life, so I guess one should accept it with grace. If there is a change in the mood of the floor, please let me know," she entreated as she led him to the main door.

The Graven
Image

It had only been six years since the Party of God had recruited him from law school. The party had promised him a political career, considerable wealth, and free access to its network television programs. He was a representative of God. He could speak eloquently about government, and the word of the Savior. It was written by the Lord himself. Why did he feel that something was not right anymore?

Clinton Stoddard watched the ash of his cigarette fall to the floor. Why did these offices never have ash trays? Surely the tobacco lobbyists offered them free to the party. These were the thoughts that entertained him. It wasn't the tower of papers before him on the desk. In his heart, he would roll them up for fireplace logs. He would make paper airplanes of them. He would donate them to an archives. The thought of looking at them seemed more than he could stand.

He could hear the phones ringing in the outer office. Who wanted to talk to him now? He had been saying the same words for six years. His rhetoric was not new. Didn't they know that the family was the core unit of American society? Didn't they know that the Constitution only served the Godly? What did he have to say to them—or to anybody, for that matter? He picked up the telephone receiver.

"This is Senator Stoddard."

"Senator, this is Keith Davis from the Washington Bureau. Congratulations on your recent victory. The party considers your win a triumph for God and the righteous. How does it feel to be a United States Senator?"

"It is an honor to represent the party from the Senate," said Stoddard, without a hint of emotion.

"We just wanted to remind you that you are bound to the party next session. We hope you will not forget this."

"I am loyal to the party and the Creator," said the Senator, as if he had dug his voice from the pit of his stomach. "I am loyal," he repeated.

His last words revolved in his thoughts long after the conversation had ended. Of course he was loyal. How dare that son of a bitch try to make him anything less? Mounds of stationery seemed to stare him in the eyes, but it was the file that tortured him. He slowly set the file before him on the desk, as if its contents were the evidence of an unfaithful wife. He wanted to open it. It would punish him, ridicule him and confuse him. He thought that it would bring him a cathartic pain, but the sensation would be numbed by his own emptiness. Now he wanted to put it back. He wanted to hide it. With a mindless motion, he opened the folder. His mind envisioned the confrontation. He thought that it would be devastating. He felt nothing.

He did not have to apologize. The press was fascinated by a story of this kind. They at least shared partial responsibility. Could he help it if his opponent's sixteen-year-old daughter got herself knocked up and nearly died from the abortion? It wasn't his fault. The press would have found out about it anyway. The party had used the information for its political advantage. That was all. No party would be so foolish as to let a Senate seat slip by. He couldn't have stopped the party anyway. He would not apologize. People were always getting themselves into trouble and then blaming someone else for the consequences. It was morality that the public wanted. Why should they elect a man to the Senate who would consent to the murder of his own grandchild? According to the laws of God, it was nothing short of murder. His secretary's voice interrupted his thoughts.

"Mrs. Bristol is here to see you. She says she has an appointment."

"I will see her," said Stoddard, as he returned the folder to his desk drawer.

The young Senator remained seated when the woman entered the room. He motioned her to a chair. "What is it I can do for you, Mrs. Bristol?"

"You can do nothing for me or my family, Mr. Stoddard," the woman said quietly. "I just wanted to tell you about my day. I picked out a bronze-colored casket today. I ordered yellow chrysanthemums for the funeral. I took the dress that my daughter is to be buried in to the funeral home. I put this visit last on my list."

"I was sorry to hear of your daughter's suicide, but your tone implies that I was in some way responsible. For certain, it was a tragedy, but I had nothing to do with your daughter's death. You blame me unfairly. If the story hadn't reached the newspapers at election time, perhaps it would not have received so much publicity. I am not an editor. I did not make the decision to publish the story on the front page. My hand did not take the life of your daughter. Your husband has been a Senator from this district for eighteen years. How did you expect the press to react? You are not naive."

"No, Senator. May I call you that? Of course I can. That is your title. No, I am not naive. For that reason, I do not need your disclaimers of responsibility for the events that led to my daughter's death. Who are you anyway? Where did you come from? My husband has been in public office since you were eligible to have a paper route, and you were right in assuming that I am not naive. Are you trying to deny that you were involved in this political maneuver?"

"Did you come here to accuse me, Mrs. Bristol? I was not involved in planting a seed of life in your daughter's womb, nor was I involved in the decision to take that life. I did not cause the infection. As for your daughter's suicide, perhaps it was the Lord's justice. Whether you know it or not, the Lord punishes those who destroy what he creates. Justice was not invented in Rome. But I will spare you the history lesson. I have nothing else to say to you. Please leave."

The woman stood up. The evening sun shone through the western windows and made the office walls appear amber. "I will leave, Senator Stoddard," she said softly. "If I had known that you were a religious man, I might have prayed for your everlasting soul. My time would have been better spent."

Clinton Stoddard watched the woman exit. Who was she to come in here accusing him? He lit a cigarette. The smoke curled around his fingers like the body of a snake. Why did he agree to talk to her? He walked toward the window. The rush hour had begun. The cars appeared as pieces of a jigsaw puzzle when the traffic stopped. Drivers were beginning to turn on their headlights, a chain reaction of thoughtless motion. An ambulance tried to make its way through the backed up cars. Its flashing lights weaved through the traffic like an electronic game. The distance between him and the street made it all seem so absurd. He walked back to his desk. He would leave when the traffic thinned out.

The party manual caught Stoddard's attention. He removed it from the shelf. This book explained his role as a party member. In the beginning, its message had created a politician from a pig farmer's son who thought he wanted to be an attorney. In his hands, it felt familiar. The softness of its worn cover made him remember that the manual contained words that he once believed. Like a student before an essay test, he tried to remember the main points. His memory was vague. He opened the book in the center, read his notes in the margin, and went on to read Matthew:

> *Do not think that I have come to bring peace on earth; I have not come to bring peace but a sword. For I have come to set a man against his father, and a daughter against her mother, and a daughter-in-law against her mother-in-law; and a man's foes will be of his own household. He who loves his father or mother more than me is not worthy of me; and he who loves his son or daughter more than me is not worthy of me; and he who does not take up his cross and follow me is not worthy of me. He who finds his life will lose it, and he who loses his life for my sake will find it.*

Memories from childhood flashed through Stoddard's mind. There was one memory that his mind would not let loose. It was the farm. A piglet born with a deformed leg, shunned by its mother, lay on the grass. In an attempt to quicken a slow death, his father crushed the animal with his boot. It was kind. No animal should starve to death. It gasped for air. Its crippled body rolled across the grass. He remembered how he wanted to save the animal. It tried to live. It wanted to live. But the boy was helpless. What could he do? As if the creature had assembled its entire energy, it gasped and was still. Why was he thinking about that? It was a scrawny runt. His father never could have sold it on the market. He would not think of it anymore. He would go home. Rush hour was over. Clinton Stoddard returned the manual to the bookcase. He would go home.

With that resolution, he saw the letter. It was marked urgent. The world believed that its cause was urgent. Was he to speak at a luncheon? Maybe the letter concerned missing prisoners or the bill on water rights. He laughed at the thought of any true urgency.

The letter was already opened. His eyes skimmed the paper. This could not be right. His concentration now followed every word. He would not go to the funeral. They could not order him to do so. He was not concerned with the party's reputation. Were they offering him as the lamb, to appease the family's vengeance? This time they were going too far. He could imagine the Bristol woman's eyes. Raw grief would be alloyed with hatred. She would know why he was there. Did the party believe that the press would attend? It was obvious to him that the family would not be fooled by such pretense. They would not want him there. It would make a mockery of the ceremony. They would accuse him and be horrified by his presence.

This was it. The party had tortured them enough. Stoddard wanted his God now. His blood felt like fire racing through his veins. His mind was blank. Fear had consumed him. He wanted to burst out of his flesh. He wanted to run. Instead, he picked up the telephone receiver and began to dial. After many rings, a voice came across the line. Stoddard began to speak.

"Fred, I just read this letter that you sent about the Bristol girl's funeral. I will not go. I can't go," he restated. "I think it is in poor taste because of the implications going around. I am sure that you have heard …"

"Look, Clinton, that is precisely the reason that you must go. The party needs a clean image. These rumors are very harmful. If you attend the funeral, nobody would have the guts to think that you were involved. You must think of the future in this situation. You can't get so emotional or it will be your downfall. The Party of God has put its faith in you. This is no time to be second guessing decisions from the top. You were instructed to attend the funeral. It won't hurt you, and you must remember six years is not a long time. The public will remember your kindness and compassion in this matter. Are you feeling better about it now?"

Clinton Stoddard replaced the receiver. What had he told Fred? Of course, he had to go to the funeral. Would they question his loyalty to the party? How could he have been so foolish?

He wished that he could cry. He could imagine the tears forming in his eyes, but they were not there. The funeral would not hurt him. Nothing could hurt him, because something told him that he was already dead. He could only wonder when it happened.

ABOUT THE AUTHOR

Mattie McClane is a graduate of Augustana College, holds an M.A. in English from the University of Louisville, and an M.F.A. in Creative Writing from the University of North Carolina at Wilmington. She is the author of *Night Ship: A Voyage of Discovery* and *Wen Wilson.*